CROWN VIC

The Dead Man Series (coauthored with William Rabkin)
Face of Evil
Ring of Knives (with James Daniels)
Hell in Heaven
The Dead Woman (with David McAfee)
The Blood Mesa (with James Reasoner)
Kill Them All (with Harry Shannon)
The Beast Within (with James Daniels)
Fire & Ice (with Jude Hardin)
Carnival of Death (with Bill Crider)
Freaks Must Die (with Joel Goldman)
Slaves to Evil (with Lisa Klink)
The Midnight Special (with Phoef Sutton)
The Death March (with Christa Faust)
The Black Death (with Aric Davis)
The Killing Floor (with David Tully)
Colder Than Hell (with Anthony Neil Smith)
Evil to Burn (with Lisa Klink)
Streets of Blood (with Barry Napier)
Crucible of Fire (with Mel Odom)
The Dark Need (with Stant Litore)
The Rising Dead (with Stella Green)
Reborn (with Kate Danley, Phoef Sutton, and Lisa Klink)

The Jury Series
Judgment
Adjourned
Payback
Guilty

Nonfiction
The Best TV Shows You Never Saw
Unsold Television Pilots 1955–1989
Television Fast Forward

Science Fiction Filmmaking in the 1980s (cowritten with
William Rabkin, Randy Lofficier, and Jean-Marc Lofficier)
*The Dreamweavers: Interviews with Fantasy
Filmmakers of the 1980s* (cowritten with William
Rabkin, Randy Lofficier, and Jean-Marc Lofficier)
Successful Television Writing (cowritten with William Rabkin)
The James Bond Films: 1962-1989
The Joy of Sets

CROWN VIC

LEE GOLDBERG

CUTTING EDGE

ISBN-13: 978-1-957868-98-1

Published by
Cutting Edge Books
PO Box 8212
Calabasas, CA 91302
www.cuttingedgebooks.com

INTRODUCTION

This slim volume contains two gritty, sexually explicit stories about an ex-con named Ray Boyd that I wrote some years ago when I was between book contracts.

I wrote the first story, *Ray Boyd isn't Stupid*, as a twist on the old *Postman Always Rings Twice / Body Heat* cliché about a guy who lets a woman get him into deep trouble. But once I finished the story, I didn't know what to do with it … or if it was any good. So, I showed it to my friend Lawrence Block, who'd just published a story of mine in one of his anthologies, and asked him if he'd give it a read.

He loved the story, and demanded that I immediately write a sequel. You don't say no to Lawrence Block, so I did as I was told and quickly wrote another one.

The second story, *Occasional Risk*, is what I like to think of as an "anti-Reacher," which is a reference to Jack Reacher, of course. I delivered it to Larry, and he liked it even more than the first one, and told me to get started right away on the next one.

But, after writing *Occasional Risk*, I'd signed a contract for two more books and wasn't sure that spending time on the side writing a third Ray Boyd story made any sense.

"I'm honestly thrilled, and flattered, that you like the stories," I said to Larry, "but what's the point of writing any more of them?"

"You're entertaining me."

"That's great, but then what do I with them? There's no market for short stories like these any more. Who will publish them? *Ellery Queen* and *Alfred Hitchcock* certainly won't."

"Who cares? If you keep this up to amuse me, one day you'll have enough Ray Boyd stories to fill a book," he said. "Then you can sell *that*."

It was an interesting thought, and I shared it, and the stories, with my agent. She liked the stories too (much to my surprise) but in her opinion, there wasn't a big market for collections of crime stories about the same protagonist... unless they were by Lawrence Block. On top of that, these stories weren't anything like the police procedurals and fun, escapist thrillers that readers expected from me... so who would buy this collection?

I thought those were good points... and, besides, I had two novels to write. So, I put the stories in a drawer and forgot about them. That was several years, and four novels, back. But recently my brother Tod asked me to consider writing another Ray Boyd story, this time for an anthology he's editing. And as soon as he said that, I heard Ray's voice speaking to me again... telling me a wicked tale of sex and violence... and I realized that I'd missed him.

Which brings me to this slim collection. I'm publishing these two stories to test the marketplace. Should I write more Ray Boyd stories? If you think so, leave me a nice review on Amazon... and if I get a strong, positive response, maybe you will see more of Ray.

Lee Goldberg
September 2023

RAY BOYD ISN'T STUPID

There weren't many cars on the highway, and what few there were quickly moved aside when they saw Ray Boyd's black-and-white, Crown Vic Interceptor screaming up behind them in their rear-view mirrors.

They thought it was a cop car, which it once was. Ray bought the huge cruiser at a police auction in L.A. because it was cheap, had a monster engine and would scare people out of his way. Besides, he appreciated the irony of driving a cop car after doing time for stealing Porsches. It reminded him of the past and what happens when you're stupid.

Ray Boyd wasn't stupid any more.

He realized in prison that all he really needed was a few bucks in his wallet and a woman every couple of days. Both came pretty easy to him. He knew he was good looking in a rugged, muscled, kind of way that would get him work and women any place he cared to stop.

And there were a lot of stops. Ever since he got out of prison, staying in one place for more than a month or so made him feel locked up all over again. So he kept moving, which also kept him from being stupid, from wanting things he couldn't have and didn't need and would never get.

What Ray Boyd wanted on that hot, dry day in July was a cheese burger. So instead of following the highway along the curve of Deer Lake, he got lured away by a faded billboard for Granite Point Park Resort and the promise of cold beer, hot food, great fishing, boats-for-rent, and ten rustic cabins amidst the trees along the shoreline.

Ray steered his Crown Vic onto the gravel road and down towards the lake, kicking up a cloud of dust and rock that momentarily obscured the billboard, and its cartoon depiction of a surprised fisherman getting yanked out of his boat by the gleeful trout on his hook.

The road crossed through a thicket of tall, overgrown trees that was bisected by railroad tracks that curved around the lake before disappearing into the forested hills. Ray caught a glimpse to his right of a rusted mobile home and a pick-up truck on blocks parked amidst the trees, both covered with a blanket of leaves.

The road spilled out into a gravel parking lot and the Granite Point Park Store, a three-story, white clapboard building that was mostly porch on the ground level and built on its namesake, allowing it to loom a bit over the lake, the dock and the beach below.

The store was the centerpiece of the park. The upper floor was a residence that didn't seem to fit somehow, as if it had been dropped on the roof by a tornado and they'd just decided to keep it there. The middle floor was the store and café, the lower level was captured space created by enclosing the pilings that held the building up. On either side of the store, set back from the shore by a dry lawn, were ten identical white cabins, five on each side, with small porches facing the water.

Ray parked his car against one of the railroad ties that marked the spots and got out. He wore a black t-shirt, faded jeans, and the pair of snake-skin cowboy boots he won in a poker game the night before his arrest.

The hot, heavy air smelled of outboard motors, lighter fluid, fish guts, and suntan lotion. Most of the cabins looked empty, a few had families camped out front, the kids running around, the saggy-breasted mothers basting on chaise lounges while the pot-bellied fathers knocked back beers and looked for teenage girls to ogle. There were a few water skiers and fishing boats on the small lake, but there didn't seem to be a lot of action. It was the kind of forested lake where people parked Winnebegos instead of building vacation homes, though there was a smattering of cabins amidst the trees.

Ray strode up to the store. The porch was lined with heavily shellacked wooden benches that faced the open counter that doubled as the store and cafe. Three old men sat on one of the benches, smoking cigarettes and nursing Cokes. They looked like they'd been installed with the benches fifty years ago. Ray nodded at them as he passed.

The store wasn't a place you could walk into and browse. All the merchandise, which was mostly groceries and fishing supplies, was on the shelves and in the iceboxes behind the open counter, which itself was a glass display case full of melting candy and fishing lures. The café was a screened-in section of the porch that faced the lake.

Ray opened the screen door, and went into the café. The seating was a half-dozen bar-stools at the counter and some shellacked picnic tables along the wooden railing.

There was a hand-painted menu above the counter and an electric fly trap in the corner that snapped every few seconds. Two kids, a boy and a girl that were maybe eight or nine years old, sat a table staring at the fly trap, letting their popsicles melt all over their bathing suits as they waited in suspense for another insect to get zapped. A HELP WANTED sign was thumb-tacked under the zapper and was caked with charred bugs.

The wood-paneled walls were plastered with layers of yellowing, loosely taped and stapled photographs of people posing with the fish that they'd caught.

Ray took a stool at the counter, with his back to the lake, and faced the parking lot, the grove of trees, and the old men, all of which he could see through the free-standing shelves of merchandise in the store.

"What'll it be?" asked a big man, who emerged from the kitchen and faced Ray on the other side of the counter.

The man wore an apron that had the same cartoon on it as the highway billboard. He was rosy-cheeked, and doubled-chinned, and appeared as jolly as a department store Santa with a body to match. But behind that avuncular smile was a hardness that Ray's prison yard antennae picked up on right away.

Don't be fooled by this guy.

Ray looked at the menu above the counter. The prices had been painted over and changed many times as the years passed, but the menu itself remained the same: burgers, hotdogs, bacon and eggs and a combination of them all called The Granite Burger.

"Cheeseburger, fries and a coke," Ray said.

"My wife's specialty," The man said and repeated the order, yelling it to someone in the dark recesses of the kitchen, then turned his gaze again on Ray, giving him a thorough appraisal.

"Something the matter?" Ray asked.

"Not at all, friend. I was just observing that you're an able-bodied young man with the sun in your face and the wind in your hair and I'm envious. It's like looking at myself twenty years ago. Heading somewhere special?"

"I'll know when I get there," Ray said.

The man laughed, took a Coke bottle out of the icebox, twisted off the cap and set it down in front of Ray.

"You're rambling man, foot-loose and fancy-free. That was my dream, too, when I was your age. Even tried it. Set out on that highway over there with nothing but a motorcycle and a few bucks in my pocket. Didn't take long for me to discover that what was out there wasn't any better than what was right here, so I came back. Of course, I had something to come back to. Not every man does." He offered Ray his hand. "Joe Bodette. Welcome to Deer Lake."

They shook hands. Joe's skin was calloused and his grip was strong. "Nice place you've got here, Joe."

The fly trap crackled and the two kids squealed with glee.

"Thank you. It's been in the family for damn near sixty years and, except for a new coat of paint every spring, and some fresh gravel on the road every now and then, it's stayed pretty much the same. People keep getting on me to add satellite TV and internet, but the hell with that, I say. I bet you get along without it. I bet you don't even own a cell phone."

"I've got no calls to make," Ray said.

"And there's nobody hounding you, checking up on what you're doing, demanding your time and attention, tying you down no matter where you are. You're a free man. Not many folks can say that. But you still have to put gas in the tank and food in the gullet."

"I've had no trouble lucking into work here and there."

"Good news," the man gestured to the HELP WANTED sign. "Your luck is holding."

"What kind of help are you looking for?"

"Washing out the boats, raking the beach, painting the cabins, replacing light-bulbs, sweeping the porch, that sort of thing. General clean-up and maintenance. "

"What's the pay?"

"Ten bucks an hour. That includes room and board. A cot in the boat house, and all your meals here at the counter, right off the menu. Eggs and flapjacks for breakfast, burgers or hot-dogs for dinner. And lake living in the summer time, which is the dictionary definition of paradise."

Ray turned around and looked down at the lake.

There were rowboats and canoes up on the sand. A boat dock, with about a dozen slips, stretched out from the shore. At the end of the dock was a tiny, wooden cabin with a corrugated metal roof, a gas pump and a metal chair that faced out towards the lake. The work didn't sound so hard and Ray thought it might be nice to sit in that chair in the evening, maybe have a beer and do a little fishing.

"Is that the boat house at the end of the dock?" Ray asked.

"It's got the nicest view in the park," Joe said.

When Ray turned back, a woman was standing in front of him holding a plate with his lunch on it. She was a caramel-skinned, full-bodied woman in her 30s, with plump lips and heavy breasts that practically tumbled out of her scoop-necked peasant shirt as she leaned down to put his sizzling burger on the counter. The view and the aroma of the charbroiled meat awakened primal hungers in him as old as man and as instinctive as breathing.

He lifted his gaze from down her shirt and saw her staring right into his eyes, all but telling him that she knew exactly where he was looking and what he was feeling.

And that she didn't mind at all.

She smiled, ever so slightly, her eyes sparkling with amusement.

Ray glanced at Joe, who'd apparently missed what had passed between them. His attention was on those kids, who'd covered their table and themselves with melted ice cream. Joe grabbed a rag and stepped out from behind the counter.

"Look at the mess you've made. Go on down to the beach and take a swim," he said, playfully swatting at their behinds with his rag as they ran out. "Give the fish something sweet to nibble on."

Joe started wiping down the table.

Ray turned back to Joe's wife. She was still standing in front of him, appraising him as openly as Joe had, so he gave it right back to her.

"You look mighty hungry," she said, absently playing with the drawstring tie that tangled from her neckline.

"I am."

"I bet you've got an appetite that's hard to satisfy."

"It's not so hard," he said.

She leaned over the counter, stole a French fry from his plate, and smiled as she glanced at his lap. "Certainly doesn't look that way to me."

She slid the French fry slowly into her mouth, turned her back on him, and went back to the kitchen, giving him the opportunity to appreciate the way her black pants hugged her.

He picked up his cheeseburger and took a big bite out of it. It was delicious. Raw, hot and moist, the juices dripping off of his chin. He thought about her lips, and her breasts, and that ass, and took another bite.

"You sure like Isabella's cooking," Joe said, stepping back behind the counter. "Stick around and you can feast on her delights every day. I don't see how you can resist."

Neither could he and that worried him.

So he quickly finished his burger, sopped up the juices off his plate with his fries, downed his ice-cold Coke, and put some cash on the counter.

"Thanks for lunch," Ray said. "And the hospitality."

"Hope you'll keep my offer in mind," Joe said, sweeping the cash off the counter into his hand. "Come back and see us real soon."

Ray strode out to his car. He was intent on leaving but had no idea where he was headed.

As he crossed the gravel lot, he spotted a woman sweeping the porch of one of the cabins. Her hair was tied back in a scarf. She wore faded blue jeans and a Granite Point t-shirt that clung to her thin body, enough for him to be sure she wasn't wearing a bra and didn't really need one. He wondered if she cleaned the boat house, too.

There were definitely some strong incentives to stick around, but there were also a lot of good reasons to get the hell out of there. If he stayed, he'd be like a lit match in front of a leaking propane tank. But the explosion sure could feel nice.

Don't be stupid.

That little voice in his head made a strong argument, so he got in his big Crown Vic, backed out in a spray of gravel, and sped off.

❧   ❧   ❧

Ray was half-way around the lake, almost at the point where the highway ambled off into the hills, when he heard the siren behind him.

He glanced into the rear view mirror and saw the green-and-white Sheriff Department's cruiser behind him. It was a newer model of the Crown Vic that he was driving. Ray pulled over to the side of the road, rolled down his window, and waited.

The deputy got out of his cruiser. He was pale-skinned and had the look of a man who'd been muscular in his 20s but who'd started letting himself go now that he was in his 30s. Ray figured the deputy would be morbidly obese by his 40s and maybe dead by fifty, if somebody didn't shoot him first.

The deputy adjusted his belt and strode up to the driver's side of Ray's car. His uniform was perfectly pressed and creased, his tie tightly knotted, his badge sparkling, but his underarms were damp with sweat, which kind of ruined the whole effect.

"Do you know how fast you were driving?"

"Nope. My eyes were on the road, not the speedometer."

"License and registration, please."

Ray reached into his pocket and pulled out his wallet, which wasn't very easy. The wallet was thin but his pants were tight. He had to hike himself way up the back of the seat to give his arm the room to maneuver. He took his license out of the wallet and handed it to the deputy, then reached slowly across the bench seat to the glove box.

The deputy tensed up, ready for action, like Ray might have a loaded .357 in there or something, but all that was inside was the registration. Besides the slip of paper, the glove box was completely empty. The deputy relaxed. Ray left the glove box hanging open and gave the registration to the deputy.

"You were going 85 miles per hour in a 65 mile per hour zone," the deputy said.

Ray shrugged. "Everybody does it."

"Please remain inside the vehicle," the deputy said and returned to his car. He sat down in the driver's seat and started typing information on his computer terminal.

Ray didn't know if it would come back that he was an ex-con or not, but he figured the deputy probably picked it up already, the same way Ray would have known this guy was a cop even if he was wearing a gorilla costume.

But there were no wants or warrants on him, so Ray didn't care what the computer said about him. He knew he wasn't going back to a jail cell.

Ray looked out at the lake. It was nice. The kind of scene he'd often imagined on those cold nights and hot days in prison. He dreamed of beaches and lakes. Places where he could relax and where the women hardly wore a damn thing.

The deputy ambled back up to his window. "I'd like to take a look inside your trunk."

"I'd like to fuck Scarlett Johansen, but I guess I'm a bit more ambitious than you."

'You got something in that trunk you don't want me to see?"

"Nope," Ray said.

"Then why do you have a problem with me taking a look?"

"You got me in kind of a logical trap there, huh? Guess I got to open it now."

"Is there anything you want to tell me first?" The deputy said. Like it was some big favor, offered by a buddy only looking out for Ray's best interests. "Anything I should know?"

Ray got out of the car. The deputy took a step back, his hand near his gun, and that amused Ray, and made him feel dangerous, so he had a cocky smile on his lips when he said:

"Just some advice. You might consider buying some antiperspirant."

The deputy smiled like he was about to shove his fist into Ray's stomach, or at least that's how Ray took it. So Ray tensed up his abs, preparing for the fist, not that he was afraid of it. He'd taken worse and hadn't shown any fear, then, either.

But the deputy didn't punch him. He just smiled back at Ray. "Open the trunk and step back from the vehicle."

Ray went to the rear of the car, unlocked the trunk, and opened it. All that was inside was a ratty suitcase, a spare tire, and a jack. He stepped back, as he was told, and leaned against the front of the deputy's car. The grill was hot, he could feel the heat through his jeans.

The deputy went back to the front of the car, opened the driver's side door and looked around the inside. He peered under the front seat, then opened the back door and repeated his actions. When he leaned out of the car, he looked at Ray and jerked his head towards the freeway shoulder. "Move over there. I don't want you behind me."

"What are you afraid I'm gonna do?"

"I won't ask again," the deputy said. "I'll just make you."

"I was only curious, no reason to get aggressive." Ray moved over to the shoulder and leaned against the low, cyclone fence between the freeway and some farmer's grazing land. From where Ray stood, he could see the lake spread out in front of him and back of the Granite Point Store. He thought about how Isabella leaned over to give him his food and how she caught him looking down her shirt and how she didn't care. He thought about how nice it would feel to bury his face between those huge breasts. And then Ray thought about Joe Bodette, and the edge he'd sensed under behind that jolly face.

The deputy rummaged around the large, empty trunk, then unzipped the suitcase. "I'm not sure that's legal," Ray said.

"Are you a lawyer?" The deputy asked.

"No."

"Then what would you know about what's legal or not?"

Ray smiled. "There you go, twisting me up with your tricky logic again."

The deputy opened the suitcase and rummaged through it. There were some t-shirts, underwear, a couple of pairs of Levis, and a shaving kit containing a razor, shaving cream, deodorant, condoms, Rolaids and some Advil. There was also a good-sized hunting knife, a Rambo special as he liked to call it, a Stephen King paperback, a deck of playing cards, and a tattered photograph of a woman standing in front of a motorhome in the desert. She was the only woman besides his mother who ever said she loved him. He abandoned her the way his mother had abandoned him.

"You travel light." The deputy said.

"I don't like to unpack."

"What do you use this knife for?"

"Flossing my teeth," Ray said.

"You in a hurry to be some place?"

"No."

"Then why were you driving so fast?"

Ray shrugged. "I like the way it feels."

"Number one reason people go fast is because they are in a hurry. Number two reason is because they are running from something," the deputy said. "Are you running from something?"

"I'd like to get the hell away from you, but I haven't got my ticket yet."

The deputy slammed the trunk closed and adjusted his belt again. "Most people get pulled over by a police officer for speeding try real hard to be friendly and respectful."

"Most people get pulled over by a police officer for speeding don't have their cars searched." Ray said. "I guess I should feel special."

"The fine is $380," the deputy said. "Payable now."

"I don't have $380," Ray said.

"Then it's going to be seven days in jail."

Seven days in a small-town jail would be a vacation compared to the several years he'd spent in the state penitentiary.

But he'd made a promise to himself and he intended to keep it. Besides, he only had $200 in his wallet.

"I got a better idea," Ray said. "You can dock my salary until I'm paid up. I'm working at Granite Point."

"So what were you doing speeding on the highway?"

"Just taking a drive around the lake to acclimate myself."

The deputy frowned. "Follow me down to the store and let's see if Joe backs up your story. Otherwise, you might be looking at a perjury charge."

Ray waited for the deputy to make a U-turn, then he followed the cruiser back down to the resort, parking side-by-side in the gravel lot. When they pulled up, Joe was bringing out fresh Cokes to the three old men.

"Afternoon, Bobby," Joe Bodette said to the deputy as he came down the steps to meet them. "What can I do for you?"

The deputy jerked his head towards Ray. "He says he works here."

"He does. Hired him this morning, " Joe glanced at Ray. "I see you discovered our little speed trap. The curve in the road pays Deputy Wheeler's salary. I should have warned you about that."

"He owes the county ten dollars a day until he pays off his fine," Wheeler said. "But he doesn't have it."

"I do." Joe said. "Why don't you sit down, Bobby, and ask Isabella to make you a milkshake while I find my checkbook."

The deputy glowered at Ray then walked past him into the café.

"Thanks," Ray said to Joe. "I appreciate it."

"No problem, I'll just dock your pay ten-dollars-a-day until we're square," Joe said with a smile. "I don't believe I got your name."

"Ray Boyd."

"Welcome to the team, Ray. I'm sure you'll end up liking it here so much you'll want to stay until we lock up for the winter. Let me set you up with a t-shirt and show you around."

Joe led him down a set of concrete steps which led all the way down to beach and docks below. But there was concrete slab landing mid-way in front of a locked door that led to a storage area underneath the store. Joe unlocked the door, hit a light switch, and Ray followed him inside.

Inside the big room, the granite cliff was exposed as were all the beams, cross-beams, and pillars that supported the store. It was like being under a railroad trestle. It was lit by naked bulbs dangling from the beams. There was no circulation, so the air was heavy, hot, and still, and smelled of dirt, dust, and aged wood. A ladder built into one of the pillars led up to a trap-door in the wood-plank ceiling that presumably led to the store.

The room was stuffed with outboard motors, boating equipment, all sorts of floatation devices, ropes, fishing tackle, tools of all kinds, bags of cements mix and fertilizer, dozens of cans of paint, boxes of grass seed, cleaning supplies, garden hoses, and big stacks of pre-cut planks of wood, presumably for repairing the docks.

"This is the supply room," Joe said as he worked a key off his cluttered ring. "Everything you'll need to do your job you'll find somewhere in here. Help yourself to a few t-shirts. That's our uniform around here. "

Joe gestured to some boxes amidst the clutter that were full of t-shirts and aprons. Ray rooted around until he found a couple of large ones.

"Your major job will be washing down the boats, gassing them up, and getting them ready for rental. Otherwise, you'll be a jack-of-all-trades, doing whatever needs to be done, and on that score, I'd like you to take the initiative. If you see a plank that's loose on the any of the boat or swim docks, fix it or replace it. A toilet overflows in the restrooms, unclog the crapper and clean-up the mess. If you see paint peeling off a cabin or picnic table, do a touch up. Kid pukes on the grass, wash off. Light bulb burns out, change it. In between, keep the beach and parking lot raked nice."

Joe snatched a key ring off a hook on the wall. The ring was full of keys that extended from retractable line to a belt-clip attachment.

"These keys will get you into the store room, the boat house, and the cabins. The numbers on the keys match the numbers on the cabins. The strange looking key unlocks the gas pump for service." He handed Ray the fat key ring. "Think you can handle that?"

"It's why I got myself that degree in rocket science."

Joe grinned. "I like you already."

⚜ ⚜ ⚜

Joe went back up to the store. Ray clipped the keys to his belt and walked around the property to familiarize himself with the resort. It was hot, he was sweating, and his shirt stuck to his skin. The maid was coming out of Cabin #3, carrying a bulging Hefty bag.

"Can I give you a hand?" he asked, but didn't wait for her to accept his offer. He took the bag from her and she let him.

She had a lithe body, like a gymnast or dancer, and looked at him with doe eyes. "I take it you're the new help."

He lifted the bag. "And here I am, helping. Where do I take this?"

She led him behind the cabin, where she had parked a small flat-bed electric cart. She tipped her head to the cleaning supplies and several trash bags in the bed. "Just dump it there. I'm Meg."

"Ray," he said, tossing the bag with the others. "What's your story?"

"Sad and boring," she said. "No education, no luck, and I clean toilets. What's yours?"

"I just got out of prison."

"What did you do?"

"Whatever I wanted."

She nodded. "I'm a drug addict. Got out of rehab then got out of the city. Figured I had a better chance of staying clean if I got away from the street. This is as far as I got."

"How long have you been working here?"

"A few months. Same deal as you, except I live in the trailer instead of a shack on the lake," she said, gesturing towards the trees and the railroad tracks. He'd seen the trailer back there when he first drove in.

"Who else works here?"

"Just Joe and Isabella," she said.

"What do you think of them?"

"They're nice enough and stay out of my way. As long as the cabins are clean and ready by 3 p.m., they don't care where I am or what I'm doing. The food is good, my trailer is comfortable, and they pay me in cash. I can't complain."

"What about Deputy Wheeler?"

"He spends a lot of time here," she said. "I suppose it's more exciting than Deerton."

"Deerton?"

"Little town up the highway. The gas station minimart and bait shop is pretty much the highlight of the town," she said. "Wheeler doesn't bother me. Does he bother you?"

"He's trying to," Ray said. "What does Isabella do?"

"She cooks some, cleans some, and is in charge of decorating the cabins, replacing dishes, linens, that kind of thing." Meg got onto the cart and eyed him. "Does Isabella interest you?"

"I just got out of prison. Every woman interests me."

Meg laughed and scooted away.

❧　❧　❧

Ray thought there was a certain cozy charm to resort, or maybe he'd just been locked up too long. It probably looked like a dump to most people. About half of the identical, one-bedroom cabins were occupied. The guests were equally divided between vacationing young families and fat retirees. The thought of ending up like any of them scared Ray more than the prospect of returning to prison.

He went back up to the store, got his bag out of the trunk of his Crown Vic and went down to the shack at the end of the gas dock. He used one of his keys on his belt to unlock the creaky, wooden door.

There was a cot, a table with two chairs, a sink and small refrigerator, a hot plate, and a small bathroom with a toilet and shower. There was a ceiling fan to churn the air when it was hot and a portable, electric space heater to fight a chill. It was a suite at the Four Seasons compared to the cell he'd been living in the last few years.

He parted the tattered curtains on the window and looked out at the Granite Point store, the beach and Deer Lake, which was about a mile long and a mile wide. It was nice, peaceful and quiet. And yet, in its own way, full of dangerous possibility.

Maybe it was that thought that lifted his gaze up to the store. He saw Isabella standing on the porch, looking down at him with her hands on her hips, a contemplative look on her face, as if she was sizing up the risks.

He knew the feeling.

⚜   ⚜   ⚜

The first two days went by quickly. He unclogged cabin toilets full of shit and tampons. He gassed up boats at the dock. He picked up dog crap and garbage in the picnic area. He raked the beach and cleaned the his & hers changing rooms. He washed the canoes, two-seater paddle-boats, and 12-foot aluminum V-hull boats that Joe rented out by the hour or by the day.

Whenever he went up to the store for his meals, he felt the heat radiating off of Isabella, though she hardly spoke to him. Joe seemed oblivious to the sexual tension, mostly because he was often busy chatting up the guests, ignoring his wife and the hired help.

After work, as darkness fell, Ray sat in the metal chair by his cabin, drank a couple of the beers he bought up at the store (where there was no employee discount), and listened to the water lap against the dock pilings.

One the third night, in the glow of the moonlight, he saw Meg, the maid, come down to the beach, strip naked, and dive into the water. She swam out to the center of the lake, floated there for a bit, then swam back to shore, got into her clothes, and went back into the woods without once looking at him.

But she knew he was watching. He thought about grabbing two beers and knocking on the door of her trailer to see if she wanted some company, but decided that was the wrong move.

He'd wait for her to knock on his door.

⚜ ⚜ ⚜

After a week on the job, Joe came down to the beach to show Ray how to make cheap boat anchors for the V-hulls. They poured concrete into empty coffee cans, and then stuck a loop of wire fencing in the center of the fill in each one. They lined the new, finished anchors by the boat dock along with the old, rusting ones.

"If someone rents a boat for still-fishing, you give'em an anchor and a thirty foot coil of rope to clip to it. Don't remind them to tie the other end of the rope to the boat, because we charge $50 for a lost rig. It's like airlines charging for suitcases. It's found money."

"Is the lake only thirty feet deep?"

"It's about a hundred feet in the middle. But no fisherman still fishes out there. They'll troll instead."

"Troll?

"Drag a baited, leaded line with a flashy lure deep behind the boat. If they are really lucky, they might hook a mackinaw." Joe said. "Last year, a guy pulled a twenty-five pound lunker out of there."

Ray was surprised there were such big fish in the small lake. "How do they taste?"

"Just like an itty-bitty rainbow trout."

"Do the restaurants pay top dollar for them?"

"Nobody buys macks for their menus. Besides, the only place to eat around here besides my store is the minimart, and they only serve what they can microwave."

"So why bother fishing for them?"

"The pleasure is in the fight, not the prize. It's like life. Living is the good part. The end is being eaten by worms in the dirt. So take your pleasure where you can, while you can."

"Sounds like good advice," Ray said. "But it could get a man in trouble."

Joe smiled. "That's the fun part."

Ray wondered how much trouble Joe got into before he settled down here. Or if Isabella was his trouble.

❀ ❀ ❀

Ray knew Isabelle was watching him. When he was scrubbing down the boats. When he was painting the cabins. And especially after a swim in the lake, when he pulled himself up on the dock and toweled himself dry. She was always on the store's porch, pretending to be doing one chore or another. But her eyes were on him, and he knew it was only a matter of time until looking wasn't enough.

Don't be stupid.

He kept telling himself that when it came to her, but he was beginning to think that maybe the stupid thing would be not taking advantage of the opportunities that were being offered to him.

He was stuck here until he paid off his speeding ticket. Why not enjoy himself? Like Joe said, he should take his pleasure where he could. That was living.

Hell, Joe was practically giving him permission to fuck his wife.

Besides, a wedding ring didn't mean anything. It was just a piece of cheap jewelry.

❧   ❧   ❧

It was twilight, two weeks after Ray arrived. The heat hung over the lake like fog. The crickets were already screaming for love in the creeping darkness.

He'd been washing down the boats for an hour, blasting off the dried fish guts and worms, caked dirt and loose sand, off the simmering metal. The combination of spraying all that water, and drinking three cokes while he did it, made him want to take a long piss. Ray went into the boathouse bathroom, unzipped his fly and was reaching into his shorts for his dick, when he looked up and out the little window over the toilet.

Meg had come down to the beach to smoke a cigarette and watch the sunset. She wore a thin, white tank top and the last rays of the sun cut right through it, so he could see the curve of her small breasts. The tips of her nipples. There was a lot of beach she could be on, but she chose this spot. Beyond Meg, up in the store, he could see Isabelle behind the porch screen. He couldn't see her face, but he knew she was looking down at his cabin. Like she had every night since he'd moved in.

Ray considered the three points of the triangle that had been created.

He considered Meg's nipples and Isabella's gaze and came up with a scenario that made him smile.

He finished, stepped back from the window and jerked himself until he was hard, and then he pulled up his Levis. His hard-on strained against his denim, creating a nice, painful bulge.

Ray found a beer in the cooler and went back outside, tipping the bottle back and taking a long drink as he emerged. He didn't look at Meg or glance up at the store. He just picked up the hose and, standing at an angle so the sun caught the beads of sweat on his naked chest and the bulge in his pants, finished washing down the boats.

He felt Meg looking at him. He felt Isabelle looking at him.

When he was done washing down the last boat, he tipped it over, so all the water with all the shit in it went between the slats of the dock into the lake. Then he took the hose and held it over his head, and gave himself a shower, soaking his skin into a shiny gloss and his pants even tighter around his hard-on and his ass. He dropped the hose, turned off the spigot, and went into his cabin.

And waited.

Ray didn't have to touch himself again to stay hard. He turned on the lamp beside the bed and closed the thin shades over the window. He started to dry himself off.

There was a knock at the door.

He opened it. Meg was standing there. Her eyelids were heavy, her cheeks flushed. There were tiny beads of sweat on her sun-browned chest. Her nipples were hard, and as big as those on a baby bottle, poking against her tank top. She tossed her cigarette stub into the lake and, without saying a word, met his gaze with her own and stepped up to him, lightly pressing the palm of her hand against the wet denim and the firm bulge beneath it. Her breath caught, her blush spread across her chest, but her gaze didn't waiver. He reached behind her and slammed the door shut.

⚜ ⚜ ⚜

The whole time he was fucking Meg, he knew the light from the lamp cast their thrusting, writhing, shadows onto the thin drapes over the window. And he knew that if someone were standing on the porch at the store, staring down at the cabin, that's what they'd see.

They fucked like wolves attacking a deer. Hungry, vicious, slaking a raging appetite. Meg wasn't the first woman he'd had since his release from prison, but it felt like it. Maybe they all would from now on. He wondered how long it'd been since she'd had a man, or if she always fucked like it might be the last time before winter hibernation.

Afterward, they didn't say a word to each other.

Meg was gone when he woke up in the morning and he was fine with that.

⚜   ⚜   ⚜

Ray was in the diner, having a hamburger for lunch, when Deputy Wheeler strode in. He wore an undershirt under his uniform, but the sweat under his arms soaked through anyway. Antiperspirant wasn't enough. Wheeler need to hot-mop his armpits with tar. He smelled like a wet dog.

Wheeler sat two stools away from Ray and smiled at Joe. It was only the three of them, but Ray felt crowded.

"How's it going, Joe?" Wheeler asked.

Joe placed a cold Coke bottle in front of Wheeler. "We've got five cabins rented and the sixth is booked. I can't complain."

Wheeler took a long drink of Coke, then: "No guests have come to you to complain about lost jewelry, credit cards or cash?"

"Nope. Why would they?"

"Because Ray is a thief, fresh out of prison, and you handed him the keys to everything." Wheeler said. "Guys like him, they need immediate gratification. He can't resist temptation."

Ray set down his half-eaten burger and dabbed at his lips with a napkin. "Stealing wallets and jewelry is not my thing. I stole cars. Porsches. Ferraris. BMWs. Muscle cars. Anything sleek, mean and fast. So far, I haven't seen anything like that here."

"You aren't likely to, either," Joe said. "You ever stole a pick-up truck? Maybe a loaded F-150?"

"Where's the fun in that?" Ray said.

Joe nodded and glanced at the deputy. "I think we're safe."

Ray grinned at Wheeler. "Especially with a top lawman like you on the job, Bob."

Wheeler gave Ray a cold stare. "It's *sir*, or *Deputy*, to you."

"Nah," Ray said. "I like Bob."

Joe spoke up. "Can you go check out cabin #6, Ray? Isabella told me before lunch that there's a clogged pipe in the bathroom that needs your attention."

"Sounds like the perfect job for you," Wheeler said to Joe. "Try not to fall in the shit."

⚜ ⚜ ⚜

Ray went down to the store room, used one of the keys on his belt to unlock the door, and got the plunger, the snake, and the tool box and lugged the heavy load all the way across the resort, following the loose, gravel roadway to cabin #6. It was the most remote and secluded cabin in the park, overlooking a tiny cove.

He set his equipment down on the porch, unlocked the door, and went inside. The first thing he noticed was that the window air conditioners were running, and had been for some time. The air was nicely chilled, and there was a flowery, soapy scent in the air. The living room had a sleeper sofa, two easy chairs, and a dining table with four chairs. The kitchen was separated from the living room by a Formica-topped peninsula with two stools.

Ray was about to check the bathroom when sensed he wasn't alone. There was a disturbance in the air. He turned to the bedroom instead. The door was ajar and the flowery scent was stronger. Perfume? Shampoo, maybe? He eased the door open with the toe of his shoe.

Isabella was naked on the bed, sitting up with her back against the headboard, her arms at her sides, her legs spread, her heavy breasts glistening with sweat, despite the cool air. She was a big-boned woman, heavy but not fat. She smiled coyly at him, trying to look sexy without realizing she didn't need to work at it.

"I'm here to clear the pipes," Ray said.

"So what are you waiting for?" she said.

❧ ❧ ❧

Isabella straddled him, her hands on his chest, watching his face, sliding up and down on his hard-on, her cheeks and chest flushed, her big breasts bouncing. Every so often she grimaced, as if it pained her not to come.

He wasn't exactly a detached observer. Every time she slid up and down on his cock, she'd clench her vaginal muscles, squeezing him as she went like she was wringing out a towel. He practically had to grind his teeth into dust to stop himself from coming.

And that made him angry.

Sure, it felt great, but he didn't like giving her that power over him. It made him feel needy, wanting and weak. So he reached between her legs, stroked her clit with one hand and mashed one of her breasts with the other, pinching her nipple as hard as he could.

Her breath caught sharply and, almost against her will, she began to grind more rapidly against him, lost in her own need, chasing her own release. He gritted his teeth, determined to ride it out, to show her who was really in command of their coupling.

She squeezed him hard inside, dug her fingers into his chest, and climaxed with a sharp gasp, pounding her hips against his, beating his orgasm out of him while she was still caught in her own.

His climax came like a gunshot, making him buck up, but she forced him down, putting all of her weight into her hands, pressing his back to the bed as she hammered his balls with her hips, pummeling every last drop out of him.

Finally, she collapsed on his chest and he had to admit their contest had ended in a draw. It was the best sex he'd had since he got out of prison.

After a few minutes, when she got her breath back, she said: "God, it was nice to fuck without a belly in the way. Fucking Joe is like fucking a pillow with a dildo taped on it."

"So why did you marry the guy?"

"Because he was nice to me and offered comfort and security when I needed it."

"But he didn't get you off."

"That used to get me off. It might still if he hadn't become a fat, mean, controlling asshole who treats me like his slave. I'm now his cook, waitress, maid and whore. What I want doesn't matter."

"What do you want?"

"Out," she said. "I want to see the world, anything but another day at this damn puddle."

"There's the door," Ray said, gesturing to it.

"It's not that easy," she said.

"Sure it is." He got out of bed and picked up his jeans off the floor. If he looked real close, he could see lipstick on either side of the open zipper.

"I don't have any money," she said. "Joe has it all. Over a hundred grand in cash in the store's safe, because he doesn't trust banks. Besides, he likes to look at his money, like Scrooge McDuck. He doles out a few bucks to me for groceries and that's it. I don't even have enough money for a bus ticket."

"Divorce him," Ray said, putting on his jeans. "You're bound to get something."

She shook her head. "You don't know the judges in this county and you don't know Joe."

"Then I guess you'll just have to live with it." Ray snatched his shirt and shoes and walked out.

"Fuck you," she said to his back.

❧ ❧ ❧

Isabella did fuck him. Four or five times over the next week (depending whether you count blowjobs or not), almost always in an empty cabin. They did it once in the woods, but getting pine needles and dirt in his ass killed his concentration. After their couplings, she always talked about how unhappy she was in her marriage. Ray was glad she wasn't thrilled with Joe, otherwise she wouldn't be riding him like a horse, but he was getting really tired of her bitching and was beginning to feel her spurs.

One afternoon, on a couch in cabin #1, she lay on top of him after she came, his dick still hard inside her.

"How can you stand it," she said. "Knowing that he's fucking me?"

"I haven't given it much thought," Ray said. "But you are his wife. Fucking him is part of the deal."

"Don't you want me for yourself?"

"I'll take what I can get."

"What if you could have it all?"

"What more is there?"

"The money," she said. "This place."

"I don't need the aggravation." He didn't love her. He wasn't even sure he *liked* her. But she was great in bed.

Ray pushed her off of him, freed his cock from her, and went to the shower. He didn't want Joe smelling her on him at dinner.

❧ ❧ ❧

Ray fucked Meg, often, too.

Sometimes she'd come to his shack after a swim, still slick and wet. It was like fucking the Little Mermaid. One night, at the end of the month, after some rigorous sex, they lay together in his tiny bed, sharing a bottle of beer.

She asked, "Why are you fucking Isabella?"

He plucked one of his pubic hairs off Meg's cheek. He wondered if she had some stuck between her teeth. "What makes you think that I am?"

"I clean the cabins. I've smelled you in them."

She'd definitely know his smell, there was no question about that. "Don't tell me you're jealous."

Meg shook her head. "I just don't see the point of taking the risk of pissing off Joe when you can have me or take your pick of the women who come up here from King City looking for a good time."

"Are there any?"

"You think guys are the only ones who like to fuck? What do you think these women want to do while their fat husbands are out fishing? You think they'd rather read Nora Roberts and fantasize about romance or have your face between their legs?"

"I'm not interested in being the Granite Point boytoy."

"Too late for that, Ray. It's already happened." She took the beer from him, finished it, then dropped it on the floor, letting it roll under the bed. The bottle clanked against the others under there. "What *are* you interested in?"

"Me and whatever makes me feel good."

"That's why I like you. You're the least complicated man I've ever met." She reached for his crotch, took him in her hand and began jerking him into a second act. "You've also got a nice cock and you know how to use it."

"It's not hard to figure out. It's not an iPhone."

"You'd be surprised."

⚜ ⚜ ⚜

Ray was busy the next day.

He helped a guest change a tire on his mini-van (the cheap, fat bastard didn't even tip him for his trouble), replaced a broken shower head in the men's changing room, mowed the grass in the picnic area, and cleaned the rat-traps of dead vermin in the trash area. He saw Isabella in the store at lunch, but Wheeler was sitting at the counter, too, so he took his hot-dog to go. Ray didn't want to risk the deputy picking up on any sex-vibe between him and Isabella.

That night, Ray was sitting on the dock, watching the bats fly low over the lake, when Joe approached, carrying two fishing poles in one hand and a cooler in the other.

"Let's go fishing," Joe said.

"I don't know how."

"It's very complicated. You put bait on the hook, drop it in the water, and wait for some dumb fish to bite it."

"You make it sound very exciting."

"What else do you have to do?"

The man had a point. Besides, he didn't actually ask Ray to go fishing, did he? It was the boss telling him what they were going to do. Ray didn't like that, but he was fucking the man's wife, so who was really in charge?

That thought made Ray feel better.

Ray grabbed a sweater from the shack and joined Joe in a row-boat with an outboard motor. He sat down on one of the benches, beside the coffee-can anchor, and they sped off into the night.

Joe held a flashlight out to him. "Point this out ahead of us so we don't hit anybody."

Ray did as he was told, but there was nobody else out on the water. Joe steered to a cove, on same edge of the property as cabin #6. He slowed to a stop and killed the motor.

"This is my favorite fishing hole on the lake," Joe said. "Drop the anchor, but don't toss it in the water or you'll scare the fish away."

Ray flicked off the flashlight, set it down, and gently dropped the coffee can overboard, hardly causing a ripple. He watched the rope unfurl on the floor of the boat as the anchor sank into the dark depths, finally hitting bottom with about five feet of rope to spare. He tied off the rope through the hole for the oar-lock so it was taut.

"Done like a pro," Joe opened the cooler, revealing a six-pack of beer, an ice pack to keep the drinks and whatever they kept cold, and a Styrofoam cup with a lid on it. He took out the cup, lifted the lid, and Ray saw it was full of worms seething in a bed of moist dirt. He offered the cup to Ray.

"No thanks," Ray said.

"You can't catch fish without bait. You run the hook through the worm, then drop your line in the water, and release the catch on the reel. Once you hit bottom, reel up a few turns and wait for the fish to bite. And when he does, you'll feel a tug. Give the line a little yank to set the hook and reel him in."

Ray pinched on a worm out of the cup, picked up one of the fishing poles, and did what he was told. He wiped the slime on his jeans, dropped the hook in the water, and released the line.

Joe baited his own hook. "What's it like stealing a Porsche and driving it?"

"It like sex, only better," Ray said. "What's it like buying a Ford F-150 and driving it?"

"Like masturbating in a recliner and being afraid your grandmother might walk in on you."

That comparison made no sense to him. "Can't say I've ever been in that situation."

Joe offered him a bottle of beer. "You don't know what you're missing."

Ray smiled and took the bottle. He liked Joe, certainly a lot more than he liked Isabella, but that wouldn't stop Ray from fucking her if he got the chance again. He didn't have to like a woman to have sex with her. He just had to like her body and what he could do with it.

Joe took a drink, then said: "I see you're sleeping with Meg."

Ray wondered what else he saw him. "Is there a policy against sleeping with employees?"

"Only for me and Isabella," he said with a grin. Was that a veiled warning? "I'd just hate to see it end badly, and for either one of you to go. I think we've got a crew here."

"You don't have anything to worry about. It's nothing serious for either one of us, just something to do at night because we're horny and bored. It's not some big love affair."

"Don't rule that out," Joe said. "Love makes a man stronger. Gives him something to live for."

"I live for myself, just like every other creature on earth."

"Maybe you do, but your generalization is wrong," Joe said. "Geese find a mate and bond for life. Same goes for coyotes, eagles and seahorses, among others."

"There are also spiders, crickets and octopuses that eat their male lovers after they fuck," Ray said, not sure what point he was trying to make, except maybe that the females of any species couldn't be trusted.

Joe found a different meaning, though. "I'd still argue the males lived for something more than themselves and mated for life. They sacrificed themselves for their mate."

"Or they were just willing to die for one great fuck."

"I wouldn't want to live my life that way."

"I'd prefer that to being stuck with one woman for my entire life." Ray wondered if they were still talking about geese and crickets or something, or someone, more specific. He didn't like talking around things. It confused him.

"You just haven't met the right woman yet. Take Isabella, for example."

I have, Ray thought. *Many times, many ways.*

Joe went on, "I told you I was a rambling man like you once. Well, that ended the day I rode my motorcycle into Billings and stepped into the diner where she was waiting tables. I got a job at the sugar beet processing plant across the street just so I could see her every day. I knew there would never be anybody else and if she'd have me, I really didn't need anything more than her, and this lake, to be happy. I convinced Isabella that the same could be true for her."

"Were you right?"

"We've been together for ten years, though to be honest with you, sometimes I worry that me and the lake aren't enough for her," Joe said. "But what more could a woman want?"

Ray could think of a hundred thousand things Isabella wanted. "Would you let her go if she wanted to?"

"I guess that'd depend if I'm a goose or a cricket."

⚜ ⚜ ⚜

The conversation drifted to cars, a subject Ray was more comfortable discussing. Over the next two hours, Joe caught two silver salmon and three rainbow trout. Ray got three hits on his line, but didn't catch anything. They came back around midnight.

"You make a fine fishing companion," Joe said to him on the dock. "We ought to make a habit of this."

"I didn't catch anything."

"Fishing isn't about catching fish, Ray." Joe clapped him amiably on the back, picked up his ice box and poles, and headed back up to the store. "It's about the camaraderie."

Ray watched him go, then his gaze shifted up to their home above the store. A light was on a window, and he could see Isabella looking down at them.

He wondered what she was thinking.

⚜ ⚜ ⚜

Ray got his answer when he walked into the storeroom the next morning. Isabella was waiting for him, and before he could say anything, she unzipped his pants, got down on her knees, and took his cock in her mouth.

She worked him good with her tongue, her teeth, and her hand, refusing to let him come until she was ready. And when she was, he came hard.

Isabella wiped her mouth across her arm, stood up and smiled at him. "I knew you'd take the initiative."

Before he could catch his breath, and ask what she meant by that, she walked out, leaving him standing there with his pants around his ankles and his dick hanging out.

⚜ ⚜ ⚜

It was the next day, when Ray and Isabella were on the floor in cabin #2, only a few minutes after he'd mounted her from behind, gripping her hair in one hand and yanking her head back as she came, that she finally suggested that he ought to kill her husband.

"It would be so easy. You go out fishing one night, hit him on the head, tangle his foot in the anchor rope, and push him overboard. You swim back and leave the boat out there. It would look like an accidental drowning."

Ray got up and sat on the couch. He wasn't surprised by her proposal. She'd been working up to it for a while. "You've given this a lot of thought."

"Haven't you?"

"Not really."

"Isn't that why you asked Joe to take you fishing?"

"He invited me," Ray said.

"But you got him to do that, which was smart," she said, buttering him up. "If nobody finds his boat out there by morning, I'll call the Sheriff and say I'm worried, that he went fishing alone and didn't come back. You can even say you saw him go out, since you sleep out on the dock, but you didn't hear him come back or see his boat in the slip."

"Then what?"

"We wait a few months, sell the place, take all the cash, and travel the world."

"You make it sound so simple."

"It is," She rested her head on his shoulder and stroked his thigh. "I love the way you feel inside me. I want it all the time. I don't think I can live without it."

She was really laying it on thick, he thought. But if she believed that she had him by the balls, that he'd been fucked into subservience and stupidity, she was wrong.

He wasn't that guy.

Ray Boyd isn't stupid.

⚜ ⚜ ⚜

That night, he lay on his cot and stared up at the rafters, watching the spiders scurry across their cobwebs, and thought about what he should do. He didn't want to kill Joe and run off with Isabella, not that he believed that was her intention. More likely, she planned to frame him for the killing somehow. It certainly wouldn't be hard for her to convince Deputy Wheeler that he was guilty.

He could warn Joe and, if Ray got lucky, the worst consequence might only be getting punched and fired. Ray could live with that.

Or Joe might not believe him, grab a shotgun or an ax, and kill Ray and Isabella for fucking behind his back in every cabin on the property.

Or Joe could confront Isabella with Ray's story. Maybe Isabella would burst into tears, say that Ray raped her, or that she caught him stealing, so he came up with this crazy story to cover his ass. Joe might believe that. Deputy Wheeler certainly would, and haul him into jail.

Those were just some of the dozen scenarios that Ray could imagine happening if going to Joe back-fired on him.

Of course, the obvious way out of this was for Ray to simply get in his Crown Vic, drive off and hope that Deputy Wheeler didn't get a warrant for his arrest that would hang over his head everywhere he went. And also hope that Isabella, bitter over his betrayal, wouldn't fabricate charges of rape or theft against him, too, in his wake.

But running away wasn't how Ray Boyd handled problems.

So that left only one option: doing the smart thing, what no man, particularly one like Ray, would ever do in a situation like this.

⚜ ⚜ ⚜

It was a weekday, and the only occupied cabin was #3. Ray was raking the beach by the swimming area, in preparation for the weekend, when he saw Deputy Wheeler walk down the boat dock and open the unlocked door to his shack.

He set down his rake, walked up the beach to the boat dock, and up to the half-open door, where he could see the deputy crouched on the floor, peering under the bed.

"Planting evidence or collecting bottles for recycling?" Ray asked.

Wheeler turned, and looked at him in the doorway, but didn't stand. "You're bad news and I know you're hiding something. Joe is way too trusting."

"That true," Ray said, stepping into the shack. "I'm banging his wife and she wants me to kill him."

Wheeler rose to his feet and hiked up his gun belt. "What the hell did you just say?"

"I'm fucking and sucking Isabella in a different cabin every day. She wants me to take her husband fishing and drown him so she can have the hundred grand in the safe and have me inside her all the time."

The deputy's face turned bright red. "You really expect me to believe that bullshit?"

"Tell Joe. And if he doesn't believe it, tell him I said she has a mole on her left thigh, and that she likes to have her nipples pinched real hard when you're eating her out and to have her hair yanked like a horse's reins when you're fucking her from behind, though he may not know about that last part. He doesn't seem to me like a guy who likes to come home through the back door."

Wheeler grabbed Ray by the front of his shirt and slammed his back into the wall. Ray let him do it, but gave him a big, goofy grin to show him how amused he was by the pathetic show of force.

"I ought to beat the shit out of you right now," Wheeler said.

"You could try, Bob. But to save yourself the humiliation of ending up in the lake with your gun up your ass, take Joe aside and tell him my story instead. If he doesn't believe it, he'll fire me and you can throw me in jail for a few weeks. Wouldn't you like that?"

The deputy thought things over for a moment, then released Ray and took a big step back, one hand on his gun, just in case Ray was getting ready to follow through on his threat. "Why are you telling me this?"

"Because I don't want to kill Joe or get framed for it."

"But you've got no problem sleeping with his wife, a woman you don't trust."

"Would you trust a woman who'd fuck the first guy who came along just so he'd kill her husband? All I trust her to do is get me off and she does that very, very well."

"You're a real prince." Wheeler spit on the floor and walked out.

"You're all class yourself, Bob."

⚜ ⚜ ⚜

Ray went to the store that night for dinner, unsure what to expect from Joe and Isabella, especially if Deputy Wheeler had already shared his story, but he didn't get a bad vibe off either one of them. Joe was as amiable as usual, chatting up two fishermen at the counter, and Isabella licked Ray's balls with her eyes as she set a plate of fried chicken down in front of him.

"I gave you the breasts," she said. "You look like a man who likes them big."

The comment was about as subtle as the blast from a double-barrel shotgun, which Ray half-expected might come at any moment from Joe, but her husband just smiled at the flirty comment and clapped Isabella on the ass.

"I do, too. Why do you think I married you?"

Joe winked good-naturedly at Ray and went back to talking with two fishermen, who were telling him about the monster mackinaw that got away from them today.

If Wheeler had already passed along Ray's warning to Joe, then Ray figured that Joe had missed his true calling. He should have been an actor. He'd have won an Oscar by now.

⚜   ⚜   ⚜

After dinner, Ray grabbed a couple of beers, walked into the woods, and knocked on the door of Meg's trailer. She opened the door. Meg was dressed in a t-shirt and loose-fitting sweatpants and seemed surprised to see him.

"Can I come in?" he asked. It was the first time he'd visited her place.

"All the way," she said with a sly grin and stepped aside. "What's the special occasion?"

The narrow trailer was a cozy space filled with pillows and lit by flickering candles. He wondered if the candles were a choice or if it was because she had no electricity. Either way, it was nice, warm and inviting.

"Maybe a bon voyage," he said.

They curled up on some pillows, opened the beers, and he told her about his conversation with Deputy Wheeler. It wasn't a long story. Afterwards, she said: "Be careful, Ray. If Joe doesn't shoot you, Isabella might."

Both of those possibilities had occurred to him. "Are you worried about me?"

She shrugged. "You're nice to have around."

"Does that mean you love the way I feel inside you and can't live without it?"

Meg laughed, nearly spilling her beer on her pillows. "Is that what she told you?"

"Is that so hard to believe?"

"Sorry, honey, but as long as I've got my fingers and a vibrator, I'll be just fine without you."

⚜ ⚜ ⚜

Ray left Meg's trailer, relaxed and sated, before 8 p.m. and was heading past the store on his way to his shack, when Joe stepped out of the darkness on the porch, holding two fishing poles and a cooler.

"I hear the rainbows are biting like crazy tonight," Joe said. "How do you feel about going out and catching tomorrow's breakfast?"

The electric snap of the fly trap caught Ray's attention. He looked past Joc and saw the shadow of Isabella, standing in the store, listening. His gaze shifted back to Joe and, for a split second, he saw the ugly sneer behind his jovial grin.

He knows.

"Sure," Ray said.

Joe handed him a fishing pole and they went down the stairs to the beach and the dock beyond.

Ray was pretty sure only one of them would be coming back to Granite Point alive.

❦ ❦ ❦

Joe didn't hand him a flashlight this time as they sped out towards his favorite fishing spot.

He doesn't want anyone to see us.

The outboard motor was loud, but Ray knew it wouldn't draw anyone's attention. Most of the lake homes were unoccupied on weekdays and there was only one guest at the resort. But even if anyone did hear it, and glanced out at the lake, all they might see in the dim moonlight was the froth of their wake.

As Joe turned the boat into the bay, Ray noticed another boat anchored in their fishing spot. Joe killed the motor and they glided to a stop alongside the other boat, another v-hull but a different brand than the ones Joe owned. Deputy Wheeler was in it, in uniform. Joe grabbed the side of Wheeler's boat and the hulls slapped together.

Ray waited, his hand on one of the long, wooden oars, ready to use it as a weapon if it came to that.

"Bobby told me you've been sleeping with Isabella," Joe said to Ray, his voice even. "Is that true?"

"You know it is. She wants me to kill you for your hundred grand." He held back the cruel urge to add, *and she wants to feel me inside her all the time.* "So, what happens now, Joe?"

Wheeler answered Ray's question. "You're going to murder Joe."

That took Ray by surprise. He assumed that *he* was the one they were planning to feed to the fishes. Ray looked back at Joe, but couldn't read his expression in the dark. "You decided to be a cricket?"

"I'm not sacrificing myself," Joe said. "I believe that you're sleeping with her, but I can't believe that she wants me dead. You're going to prove it to me."

Wheeler said, "I borrowed this boat from Frank Pell's cabin, which is vacant during the week." He gestured to a cabin on the other side of the cove. "You're going to swim back to Granite Point, just like you would have if you'd killed Joe. There's a dry set of your clothes and a pair of your shoes in a plastic bag under the deck of Cabin #6. There's also a keyfob-sized digital recorder in pocket of your pants. Joe will leave his boat here and come back with me to Pell's place, where I've got my car."

"So you want me to go back to the store and get her to incriminate herself," Ray said.

"If what you say is true," Wheeler said, "that shouldn't be too hard."

It wasn't exactly *Mission Impossible*. "Then what happens?"

"We show up and confront her," Wheeler said.

"Are you going to arrest her?"

Joe leaned towards him, so Ray could see the undisguised loathing on his face. "It's none of your fucking business what we do. You won't be here. You're leaving tonight."

"Alive and in one piece?"

Joe waited a long moment before answering. "Of course. What kind of men do you think we are?"

"But don't ever come back," Wheeler added. "Or you'll get the beating you deserve."

That was fine with Ray. He didn't care how Joe resolved things with Isabella. But he was glad he wouldn't have to testify in a trial. He didn't want to ever be in a courtroom again.

⚜ ⚜ ⚜

The water was freezing, but other than that, the swim back to shore wasn't so bad. He arose from the water, shivering, and made his way up the beach and through the woods to Cabin #6. He found the black Hefty bag under the deck and cursed that asshole Wheeler for not including a towel with the dry clothes.

Ray stripped, shook himself like a dog, and got dressed, transferring his wallet, belt and the belt-clipped Granite Point keyring from his wet pants to his new pair. The digital recorder was in a front pocket of his dry pants, just like Wheeler, the Deer Lake Columbo, said it would be. He tested the device by saying a few words and playing it back:

"Ray Boyd isn't stupid."

It worked fine.

He stuffed the wet clothes into the Hefty bag, cinched it shut, and headed along the gravel path to the store. He figured that Joe and Deputy Wheeler had plenty of time to take the boat back where the Pell place and drive over to Granite Point, park the police cruiser out-of-sight, and creep up on the store themselves.

Ray was still wet and cold, his shirt sticking to his skin, and he thought about how warm and comfortable it would be if he went to Meg's trailer and nestled with her in her pillows. His gaze drifted to his right, to her trailer in the trees, and he saw the soft glow of her candles behind the drawn drapes. The urge to go there was tempting, if only to warm up, but his desire to live, and get the hell away from this goddamn place, was much stronger.

The store was dark, lit only by the occasional spark of a fly or moth getting killed in the electric trap. He stepped onto the porch, aware of every creak his weight made on the old boards. The restaurant door was unlocked. He reached into his pocket, clicked on the recorder, and went inside.

He dropped his Hefty bag on a table and stepped behind the counter into the store. The stench of years of French fry oil and burger grease, caked on the ceiling walls and floors, filled his nostrils. His stomach growled, his primal urges awakened.

Isabella peeled out of the shadows of the kitchen. She wore the same peasant top as the first day he'd seen her.

"Is it done?" she whispered.

That wasn't very incriminating and he wasn't sure if the recorder in his pocket picked it up. "Is what done? Did I plunge the toilet in cabin three? Clean up the dog shit in the picnic area?"

"Is Joe ever coming back?"

"Not unless Stephen King knows his shit and that'd be terrifying."

"Who is Stephen King?"

"Never mind," Ray said. "Let's see the money you promised would be ours when he's dead."

"What's your hurry?"

"I've never seen a hundred grand in cash."

"Taking a look couldn't hurt," she smiled, turned to a counter, and opened a cabinet door below, revealing a safe hidden inside.

"Neither would taking a few dollars now," Ray said. "It's not like anybody besides the two of you were keeping count."

"That's true," She crouched down to open the safe so she didn't see Wheeler, hunched low, creep onto the porch outside. But Ray did. She worked the dial as she spoke, hiding the combination from him with her body, then opened the safe. "The problem, though, is that you're supposed to be nearly broke."

The open door of the safe blocked his view of the interior. She reached inside and pulled out a thin packet of bills, held together with a rubber band. "This has to go back. You don't want Deputy Wheeler or anybody else finding extra cash on you. It will create suspicion that Joe's accident was murder."

She tossed it to him. He caught it and feathered the bills. It was all hundreds, maybe two or three grand. It was exciting to hold.

"Oh the hell with it," she said. "You can keep it."

"What changed your mind?' He looked up and saw Isabella standing now, aiming a gun at him.

"Because it will help convince everyone that you killed Joe and came back here to rob the safe. I caught you in the act, you tried to attack me, and I shot you."

"Uh-oh." Ray said. "I guess I'm not the mattress stallion I thought I was."

"Mattress stallion? Jesus, what a dumb-fuck you are."

"I knew that's what you thought of me. So I invited company."
He whistled and Deputy Wheeler came into the store from the
restaurant, his gun drawn. Ray reached into his pocket and held
up the digital recorder. "And it won't be your word against mine,
you greedy bitch."

"It's over, Isabella," Wheeler said. "Give your gun to Ray, butt
first."

She did as she was told. The instant the gun was in Ray's
hand, she took a big step away from him, as if he might strike
her and said, "It isn't loaded. We'll put bullets in it when you're
dead."

We'll?

Ray realized he'd been played at about the same instant
Wheeler pivoted away and aimed his gun at him.

"We've been waiting for a dumb fuck guy like you to come
along for months," Wheeler said. "But we never expected someone so perfect for the job." Wheeler backed over to the safe, took
a peek inside, and grinned. "Damn, that's sweet."

Isabella still faced Ray, who was desperately running options
through his mind. Make a grab for Isabella and use her a shield?
He didn't think he could get to her before Wheeler shot him, but
what other choice did he have?

"I take it that Joe is fish food," Ray said, trying to buy time,
to think of another play.

"They're getting their revenge now, that's for sure," Isabella
said. "You want to know what happens next?"

"Sure," Ray said. The fly trap snapped. He knew how the
insect felt.

"The story will be that Bobby caught you forcing me to open
the safe. He had to shoot you to save my life. Later, they'll find
out that you drowned Joe, too. Bobby will be a hero and we'll be
set for life."

Wheeler stepped up behind her. "There's just one tweak to
the plan that I'd like to make, honey pie."

Before she could ask what it was, Wheeler slit her throat with Ray's knife, a geyser of blood spewing onto Ray.

Isabella dropped to the floor, her eye wide with terror. Wheeler looked down at her. She jerked like fish, her throat yawning open like gills. "The tweak is that Ray killed you and ran off with the money before I got here. I was devastated when I found your body."

Ray had no sympathy for Isabella. The bitch deserved it. He wiped her blood off his face with the back of his hand and looked at Wheeler, who grinned and dropped the knife on the floor. Ray's gaze settled on the knife at his feet. He figured Wheeler must have stolen it when he was going through the shack. Or maybe he went back for it tonight, before coming to the store. It didn't matter now. It was what it was.

Wheeler gestured to the knife with a wave of his gun.

"You want to go for it, Ray? Maybe you can get to it and stab me before I blow your head off. Or maybe you can try and rush me. What have you got to lose?"

Good point.

He lunged for the deputy, who drew a taser with his free hand. Ray felt a thousand needles stab him, lost total control of his body, and fell on top of Isabella.

Wheeler kicked him in the head and everything went dark.

⚜ ⚜ ⚜

When Ray woke up, his head throbbed and his whole body itched, but there was nothing he could do about it. His nostrils were filled with the smell of the fish guts, motor oil, and sand that his head, sticky with Isabella's blood, had been laying in on the bottom of a moving V-hull boat. His hands were bound behind his back with duct tape and he could see that his ankles were tied together with the end of the anchor rope.

Wheeler sat in the stern, one hand steering the outboard motor, looking ahead into the night, so Ray was directly in his field of vision. He didn't say anything to Ray until he stopped the boat. He stood up, tossed the anchor can into the water, then lifted Ray's legs over the edge of the boat. The rope was quickly unfurling beside Ray's body.

"I was just thinking, Ray, that nobody will miss you, that your life amounted to nothing. But that's not true. Your entire purpose for being born, for existing on this earth, was to make me rich. Funny isn't it?"

Ray had nothing to say to that because his mouth was taped shut. The rope suddenly went taut, tugging hard on his ankles. But he felt a little give there, too, the rope catching on the protrusion of his fibula. Wheeler put his hands under Ray's armpits and hefted him up. Ray drew in a big breath through his nostrils.

"Now you can die knowing what you lived for."

Wheeler tossed Ray overboard.

⚜   ⚜   ⚜

The tape on Ray's mouth came off as soon as he hit the water, but the binding on his wrists held tight.

The water was ice cold and pitch black, and it felt like monster reached up from the depths, grabbed him by the ankles, and was yanking him down to eat.

The roar of outboard motor faded away, replaced by the echo in his head of his own pounding, desperate heart.

He was sinking fast and knew he only had seconds to live. His chest ached for air, and the urge to breath would soon be undeniable. And with it, so would his death.

His set of keys, dangling from the chain at his belt, brushed against the back of his hand. He managed to snag the chain with his fingers, then sorted through the keys to find the one with most serrated teeth.

Ray starting sawing at the tape with the key while it felt like another creature was inside his chest, like that thing in *Alien*, trying to claw itself out, his talons scraping against the back of his sternum. He could almost hear the scratch of the claws against the bone.

The tape tore around his wrists. He tried using his arms to swim up, but quickly realized he couldn't fight against the pull of the anchor. His chest was tearing. The urge to breath was unbearable.

Ray hiked up his knees, and reached for his shoes, untying the laces. He pulled off the shoes, straightened his legs again, pointed his feet down, and the ropes slipped off ankles, pulled away by the anchor.

He was free. But it was too late. He had to breath.

His mouth opened against his will and just as he was about to inhale water, felt lips against his own.

Meg.

She held his head in her hands and breathed into his mouth. Then, together, they kicked their way to the surface.

They broke through into the night and Ray began to gag, desperate for air. Meg held his head above water.

"Relax, Ray," she demanded. "Breathe easy, or you're going to swallow more water than air."

He felt a stabbing pain in his chest with each breath, but he couldn't suck in enough air to satisfy his need.

But after a few seconds, feeling her naked body against him, his panic eased.

You're alive.

Ray looked for the shore. He could see the Granite Point store, maybe a hundred and fifty yards away. Wheeler was on the dock, heading for Ray's shack, probably to clear out his belongings.

He looked back at Meg, his teeth chattering in the frigid water, and wondered why she wasn't cold, too. That wasn't all he wondered. "How did you find me?"

"I was in the trailer when I saw you walk to the store. I followed you," she said. "I waited and saw Wheeler drag you to the boat and head out. So I stripped and swam after him. He didn't see or hear me coming. I got here just as he dumped you overboard. Still, it was pure luck I found you."

Ray watched Wheeler emerge from the shack with his suitcase.

What was the asshole's plan?

He knew Wheeler left his car at Pell's vacant lake house and borrowed his boat to meet with Joe and Ray. So after he'd drowned Joe, he'd probably used the same boat to go to Granite Point. Now he'd have to take the money from the safe and ditch Ray's Crown Vic somewhere temporarily until he could get rid of it for good.

Ray could only think of only one logical place to do that.

⚜ ⚜ ⚜

Meg swam back to Granite Point, where Ray told her to stay in her trailer and not come out until either he came to her door or the Sheriff's deputies showed up.

Ray swam toward the Pell's place. He hoped that hypothermia or exhaustion wouldn't drown him before he got there.

⚜ ⚜ ⚜

His burning rage probably kept him alive. He pulled himself up onto the dock and, soaking wet and shivering, he trudged up the overgrown, weedy lawn to a small cabin with a screened-in porch. The whole place looked as if it was built without a blueprint and using scrap wood, a do-it-yourself project completed room-by-room by an amateur who didn't own a level.

Ray crept around the edge of the cabin and saw Wheeler's Crown Vic cruiser parked behind a lopsided, standalone garage, hiding the vehicle from sight by anybody passing by on the narrow, two-lane road that ran along the lake.

As he was noticing that, his own Crown Vic came down the slight incline to the cabin and stopped in front of the garage. Wheeler got out, opened the trunk of his cruiser, and pulled out a set of bolt cutters. He cut the pad-lock on the garage, lifted up the door, then got back into Ray's car and drove it inside.

That's when Ray, dashed to the side of the garage, and waited. A moment later, Wheeler emerged, holding a bulging Hefty bag in one hand and the bolt cutter in the other.

Ray jumped out of hiding with a vicious growl, his hands raised like claws. Wheeler recoiled, his mouth opened wide in sheer horror, unable to even summon the air to scream at the soaking wet corpse that had come for him.

It was some serious Stephen King shit and Ray loved it.

Wheeler dropped everything and fumbled for his gun. Ray punched him in the gut, yanked his arm behind his back, and drove him head-first into the bumper of the squad car.

Wheeler dropped to the ground, unconscious.

Ray opened the trash bag. It was full of cash. He carried the bag to his car, opened the trunk, and saw his suitcase. He emptied his clothes from the suitcase, put what he estimated was maybe $25,000 in cash inside, and closed it up. He put the trash bag with the rest of the money in his trunk, closed it, and carried the suitcase over to the squad car.

He dropped the suitcase into the trunk, and spotted a box of rubber gloves, probably for use at crime scenes or dealing with people who were bleeding.

How thoughtful.

He put on a pair of gloves to cover his prints, placed the bolt cutters back in the trunk, and then took the car keys out of Wheeler's pocket.

The crotch of Wheeler's pants were soaked with piss and it smelled to Ray like the deputy might have crapped himself, too.

Serves the asshole right.

He dragged Wheeler around to the front, passenger side of the squad car, and opened the door. Wheeler's official, Trooper-style hat was on the seat.

Ray put the hat on his own head, then lifted Wheeler into the seat. Wheeler mumbled something, so Ray slammed his forehead against the dashboard to keep him out cold, then made sure the deputy was slumped far enough down in the seat that he wouldn't be seen through the window.

He went back to the garage, looked around, and found a pair of galoshes. They were a tight fit, but it was better than being barefoot. He closed the garage door, looped the broken pad-lock through the latch, got in the driver's seat of the cruiser, and drove out.

⚜ ⚜ ⚜

Ray drove to Granite Point, made a U-turn in front of the store, then sped out again onto the highway, making a hard, screeching right, nearly getting T-boned by an SUV heading the opposite direction.

That was intentional. He wanted the cruiser to be remembered, speeding away from the resort.

The Crown Vic fish-tailed as he regained control, and then he charged up behind a slow-moving motorhome. He passed the RV too close, nearly shearing off the their side-view mirror, and giving the startled, elderly driver a good look at his dark profile, before racing wildly ahead into the next curve.

Ray took the curve down the middle, crossing the center divider, forcing an on-coming Impala to swerve to avoid a head-on collision. The Impala's headlights swept quickly over the cruiser, giving the driver a quick glimpse of a man with the distinctive, trooper's hat at the wheel.

Perfect.

Ray reached the spot where Wheeler had pulled him over, crossed the median again, making sure to burn rubber over the asphalt, leaving behind a black streak that was like an arrow, and barreled towards the lake.

Just before the car reached the embankment, he tossed his hat on Wheeler, opened the driver's side door, and jumped out, hitting the dirt hard and rolling into the brush. The cruiser flew off the embankment and splashed hard into the lake, water rushing into the vehicle through the open door.

Ray scrambled deeper into the brush just as the motor home he'd passed came to a stop on the road above. He snuck away unnoticed as a man rushed out of the RV, dove off the embankment, and swam to the sinking cruiser to rescue the driver.

Ray went back to Meg's trailer and sent her to Pell's place for the Hefty bag full of trash. Now all he had to do was wait.

⚜ ⚜ ⚜

After all the years Ray had spent in prison, he didn't mind being cooped up in her trailer for a week. It was cozy, there was plenty of food and beer, and he had the $78,000 to keep him warm when Meg wasn't around.

On the night of the killings, the authorities found Isabella's corpse and the open, empty safe. The next day, they found Joe's boat and divers recovered his body. They also found Pell's boat on the Granite Point beach and went to his cabin, where they found Ray Boyd's car in the garage (but not a Hefty bag full of cash).

The Sheriff questioned Meg at the store. He had no reason to come to her trailer. She wasn't a suspect. She was the only surviving employee and possible witness of the events leading up to the robbery and murders.

Ray knew there wasn't any reasonable, or even coherent, explanation that Deputy Wheeler could give that wasn't incriminating for speeding away from Granite Point with a suitcase stuffed with $25,000 in the trunk of his cruiser. So the Sheriff quickly came to the obvious conclusion that Wheeler murdered Isabella and Joe for their money, and had planned to pin the crime on Ray, who he'd probably killed, too. Wheeler's mistake was that he'd panicked, he was frantic to get away from all the killing he'd done.

Divers searched the lake for Ray's body but, after a week, they gave up looking and everybody but Meg went away.

⚜ ⚜ ⚜

A few days after the deputies wrapped up their work, Meg and Ray left the abandoned resort in her ten year old, rusted-out, Toyota Corolla and headed to Las Vegas.

They got a room at the Bellagio, but they didn't gamble. They both figured they'd used up all of their luck at Granite Point. So they did some shopping, saw some shows, ate some great meals, and exhausted themselves with sex. Ray also found a guy to make him some fake IDs, and legitimate credit cards under the same fake names, for five grand.

On the fourth morning, after they'd finished their room service breakfast, and were sitting at the table in their plush bathrobes, Meg said it was time for them to go their separate ways.

"I don't love you, you don't love me, and I'm getting restless."

He was fine with that because he felt the same way. "What are you going to do?"

"I don't know, except that I don't want you to be part of it. You're too much trouble," She said. "No offense."

Ray held up his hands. "None taken."

That was true.

They divvied up the money that was left fifty-fifty, kissed good-bye, and then he took a taxi downtown to find a used car lot, where he bought a new ride for $1000 cash and no questions asked.

It was a black Crown Vic. A former cop car. It felt right.

Ray was on the road again within an hour, heading east. He had no idea where he was going next, but he knew he'd do just fine.

Because he wasn't stupid.

OCCASIONAL RISK

Ray Boyd was in a bathing suit, reading a Lee Child paperback, on a chaise lounge beside the swimming pool in the Copper Oasis Motel parking lot.

He was the only guest at the pool that late afternoon. That's because it was still 103 degrees outside and he was in Helmsby, a dry patch of desert off Interstate 10, forty-five miles southeast of Tucson, Arizona.

Helmsby may have been a town once, but now it was only an exit, the place where bald tires and rusted RVs went to die, and people only visited if their cars broke down, or they were desperate to piss, shit, gas-up or sleep on their way to someplace, anyplace, else.

That's why Ray, on a whim, had pulled off the freeway for a day or two of desert sunshine, something he'd missed during the years that he was in prison. He knew he'd be pretty much alone here, and that nobody here would look twice at the fake driver's license that identified him as "Bill Wyatt." He'd bought the license, and a legitimate credit card to go with it, in Las Vegas, along with a few spares under other identities.

The motel was one of three on the street, separated by a gas station, the Chuck Wagon restaurant, and a junkyard. It was a one-story cinderblock building with a flat, white gravel roof and was laid out in a half-circle around a crumbling asphalt parking lot. There was a single, sickly palm tree and a tall cactus outside of the front office, where a display spindle of ancient, Kartchner

Caverns State Park brochures were yellowing and becoming brittle behind the window.

If Ray peeked over the edge of his paperback, he could see his 2007, black-and-white Crown Vic, an old Police Interceptor that was parked directly outside of his room and had $35,000 in stolen cash hidden behind the door panels. To his right, he could also keep an eye on the frontage road, and the Interstate behind it, not that anybody was looking for him. As far as the world was concerned, he was dead, killed by a sheriff's deputy in Washington state, but it paid to stay alert.

Regardless, he would have noticed the dirt-caked, bug-spattered, red 2019 Mercedes SLC that came to a hard stop at the front office, kicking up a cloud of dirt in its wake. It was a tiny convertible, a toy that the Germans used to make for people who couldn't afford to drop $100K on a real SL. He hated the car but he immediately liked the woman who climbed out of it. She was a pony-tailed, bottle blonde in sunglasses, wearing tight, designer jeans with designer tears, and a spaghetti-strap, white tank top that clung like shrink wrap to her wash-board stomach and impossibly round and unnaturally firm breasts. She pulled a big, brown Louis Vuitton bag out of the car, slung it over her shoulder, and went inside. He only knew the brand of the bag because the logo was repeated a thousand times all over it, just so everybody would know she had money.

Ray shifted his attention back to his book. It was about Jack Reacher, a bad-ass ex-Military policeman who wandered aimlessly around the country with only a toothbrush in his pocket, helped people in trouble, solved crimes, and easily beat the shit out of anybody who braced him. Ray liked Reacher's lifestyle, and thought he could live that way, too, minus the heroism and fights. He decided that he might be able to learn a few things from the book and the others in the series.

The woman came out of the office and looked at the motel, her eyes settling first on a room across the parking lot from his, and then on him. He was tan, from a few months working outdoors at a lakeside resort, and in good shape, not gym or prison weights, but from manual labor, the right genes, and a sensible diet.

She got in her car, drove slowly across the parking lot to her room, directly across the parking lot from his, and got out again, popping the trunk to remove a big suitcase. When she shut the trunk, he noticed her clean, white California license plate, then her tight ass as she wheeled her suitcase into her room. It had only been a few days since he'd had a woman but it felt like months, particularly after becoming accustomed lately to daily, if not twice daily, action. But that had been a unique situation.

Ray set the book aside and dove into the pool, which was lukewarm but still refreshing. He did a few laps, and when he raised his head again, he saw the woman standing beside his chaise lounge, holding his paperback. She was in a yellow bikini, her tiny top barely containing her breasts, which were like two cantaloupes. He didn't find her implants attractive, but he liked everything else about her.

"Is this book any good?" She asked with a Texas twang. He liked that, too.

Ray stood up in the pool, so he was eye-level with her crotch, which he suspected was intentional. He felt a stirring in his shorts. "I found it in my room but it's given me a whole new perspective on life."

She studied him for a moment. She seemed genuinely perplexed. "Are you serious?"

"I am."

"Usually they leave a bible in your room for that."

"It's there, too, but I won't read anything that doesn't have Stephen King's recommendation on the cover."

Darlene glanced at the cover again. "Maybe I ought to read this."

"I'd be happy to read it to you," he said. "It makes a great bed time story. "

She laughed, tossed the book and her towel on the chaise lounge, and stepped into the pool, stopping a few feet away from him. "You're very sure of yourself."

"I was meek until I started reading that book."

"You don't look meek," she said.

"How does meek look?"

"Less excited."

She dove in the water and swam to the deep end. Ray wasn't the least bit ashamed of being hard. He owned it.

He leaned back against the edge of the pool and watched her swim laps. "Where are you headed?"

"To a new tomorrow. You?

"Away from yesterday."

Nobody talked like that, except in a movie, but he was playing along, curious where this was headed, his erection tenting his shorts.

She came to a stop in front of him and stood up. "It seems we've met in the middle."

"Is that what we're doing? Meeting?"

She looked him in the eye, stepped closer, and grabbed his hard-on in one hand. He didn't flinch.

"You tell me."

She smiled and began jerking him off. He met her unwavering, playful gaze, reached between her legs and began fingering her. Her breath caught for an instant, but otherwise she just kept her hand going, maintaining eye contact.

He knew it was a ridiculous scene out of a terrible porn movie and yet there they were, two total strangers, face-to-face in a pool, giving each other hand-jobs two minutes after they'd met. This didn't happen in real life, which only underscored how false and desperate the moment was, which merited some serious thought, which he'd be sure to give it after he came.

Over her shoulder, he saw a chubby, chalk-white adult couple in bathing suits and flip-flops emerge from a motel room with their two chubby little kids, who each had yellow duck-head floaties around their waists. They started heading across the parking lot toward the pool.

Ray quickened his finger-work. Her eyelids fluttered and she used her free hand to brace herself against the edge of the pool beside him. She pumped him harder and faster, demanding his climax and testing his self-control.

He gritted his teeth, shifting his gaze between her eyes and the nearing family, and tried to hold back the mounting pressure building in him.

Her mouth parted, her breathing deepened, and he smelled her minty breath. She'd used mouthwash before coming to the pool. That was interesting to him, something else to consider when he was capable of thinking again. Her legs began to shake and he knew it was over for her.

She came in a sharp shudder that flushed her face, forced her eyes closed, and stiffened her nipples. He stopped resisting the excruciating tension, releasing himself into her firm grip with an involuntary groan, his buttocks tightening with each deep pulse of his climax.

Ray removed his hand from between her legs as the family arrived at the pool.

"It's a pleasure to meet you," he said.

"Likewise."

She let go of him, and he swam past her to the deep end, where his hard-on could ebb before anyone might notice it.

She took his place with her back to the wall and rested her arms on the rim, which pushed out her flushed breasts, her nipples hard enough to hang a couple of coats on.

The chubby husband took a look at her and stubbed his toe on the end of a chaise lounge, dropping their towels on the ground.

"Fuck!" he yelled, hopping on one foot.

The chubby wife, in a floral, one-piece bathing suit, knew exactly why her husband had injured herself, and glared at the woman in the pool, who shrugged as if to say, I can't help it if I'm hot. The little girl in a one-piece tutu bathing suit shrieked with delight.

"Daddy said a no-no. We get ice cream!"

Her little brother shrieked, too. "With sprinkles!"

That little scene was more than enough to make Ray's dick go limp. He tread water and considered things. The woman's mouthwash was premeditation. She came to the pool for a seduction. But he wasn't stupid. He knew he wasn't irresistibly attractive to women and that she wasn't sex-crazed. She needed him for something besides getting off and didn't have time to waste getting his full attention, so she went straight for his dick. That would make most men her pet, but Ray wasn't most men and he'd been in a similar situation before. It nearly got him killed. But he was curious what the twist was this time.

The Chubby Husband sat on the edge of his chaise, draped a towel over his waist and massaged his injured toe while he wife led their kids into the pool. The man tried not to look at the woman in the bikini but didn't have the will-power.

Ray swam over to her. "Are you hungry?"

"Ravenous."

"Give me twenty minutes to shower and get dressed and I'll buy you dinner.

Ray got out of the pool, and she followed right behind him. He slipped his wet feet into his running shoes, and grabbed his paperback and room key from the chaise. He didn't have a towel. She wrapped a towel around herself, slid her feet into a pair of flip-flops, and hooked her arm through his as they walked away.

"I'm glad we took the edge off," she said. "We can go slow next time."

And with that tease to set her hook, she let go of him and went to her room. He watched after her for a moment, admiring her ass, then went inside.

The room was a pit, everything bolted down except the pillows, sheets, and chairs around the table. He showered, shaved, and put on a clean black t-shirt, jeans, and a new pair of black Nikes that he'd bought in Las Vegas.

He stepped outside at 6 p.m. and saw her leaning against the porch pillar beside his door. She wore high heels, another pair of pre-torn jeans, and a loose-fitting, untucked blouse unbuttoned to show off her cleavage. The big Vuitton bag was over her shoulder. He noticed now that it seemed over-stuffed and heavy.

She said, "I'm Darlene."

"I'm Wyatt."

"I'd shake your hand, Wyatt, but we've already shaken each other pretty hard."

"We certainly have."

Behind Darlene, in the parking lot pool, Ray could see the chubby wife sitting on the steps in the shallow end, watching her kids play and her chubby husband stealing glances at Darlene.

Darlene nodded at his Crown Vic. "Are you driving?"

"We're walking. The restaurant is right next door."

She seemed relieved and they began walking. "Are you a cop?"

There was no mistaking that his car had one been a police cruiser, so it was a natural question. He shook his head.

"I just like their Crown Vics because they've got big engines, they're indestructible, and everybody moves out of my way when they see me coming in their rear-view mirrors."

"So what do you do?"

"Nothing."

"How do you making a living?"

"I'm independently wealthy."

Darlene tipped her head to the front office as they passed it. Dead flies covered the window sill, fried to death by the desert sun. "Is that why you're staying here?"

"I'm frugal and it doesn't take much to satisfy me."

She smiled. "We'll be testing that theory later."

There it was, another tease. She really wanted to be with him tonight. He wondered why. It certainly wasn't for his body or his sexual prowess. Anybody with a finger, even the Chubby Husband, could do what he did to her.

"What brings you here?" Ray asked as they walked on the cracked sidewalk. He could feel the heat coming off the asphalt roadway.

"I got tired of driving and didn't want to fall asleep at the wheel."

"There are nicer hotels in Tucson."

"I would have ended up in a drainage ditch before I got there."

So she was heading west, he thought, probably from Texas, given the twang in her voice. It made him think again about her clean, California license plate. "You don't seem very tired to me."

"I've been reinvigorated."

They reached the Chuck Wagon restaurant. There was a hitching post outside, in keeping with the theme, and a western-style false-front on the building that was undercut by the glass doors and cheap windows that looked like they'd been repurposed from a motorhome. Ray opened the door and they went inside.

The only nod to the western theme here was yellowed wallpaper depicting various rodeo scenes. There were half-a-dozen red vinyl booths, common to diners everywhere, along the wall and another half-dozen tables in center of the room with checkered table clothes. In the center of each table were two bottles of wine, salt, pepper, catsup, mustard and A-1 Steak sauce. There were three other couples in the restaurant, all in their sixties or seventies. The waitress who greeted them was young and skeletally thin with long, stringy hair. Ray pegged her for an addict of some kind, crack or meth. He would be, too, if he had to live here.

"Take any table you like," the waitress said.

Ray picked a booth in the back, facing the front door. Darlene slid in first and he got in across from her. The waitress gave them sticky, laminated menus.

Darlene set the menu aside. "Can I see your wine list?"

The waitress pointed at the two bottles on the table. "That's the list. A red and a white."

"I'll take the biggest steak you have, medium rare, with a Caesar salad and a martini, dirty."

"We don't have a bar," she said. "We've got wine, Bud, Bud Light, soft drinks, Hawaiian punch, milk and chocolate milk."

"I'll have the bottle of red," Darlene said.

The waitress shifted her gaze to Ray.

He gave her his menu. "I'll have the same."

Seeing all the bones poking against her skin, Ray was tempted to buy a steak for her, too, but decided she probably wasn't interested in any sustenance that she couldn't stick in a vein. The waitress walked away and came back a moment later with steak knives and two wine glasses.

Darlene asked, "Do you have a cork screw?"

The waitress picked up the bottle of red wine, unscrewed the top, and set the bottle down in front of Darlene. The waitress walked away.

Darlene smiled at Ray. "Fancy place."

"It was this, Dairy Queen, or the microwave at the gas station mini-mart."

"Then I guess you made the right choice."

Ray studied her for a moment. "What do you do for a living?"

"I'm like you," she said. "Independently wealthy."

"Are you in hurry to get where you're going?

Darlene poured them both some wine. "I'm tired of waiting for my future and want to get there already."

"The thing about the future is that it's always gonna be in front of you."

"That, smartass, entirely depends where you're coming from. Some pasts have no future. Like mine and the one I guess you're leaving behind."

Ray nodded. "You have a point."

She held up her wine glass, he held up his, and they clicked them.

"Fuck the past, hail the future," she said.

"I can drink to that."

Darlene took a sip and so did he. It tasted like a sugary, fruit-flavored "juice" with a hint of cough syrup.

"This tastes like the Hawaiian Punch," Darlene said, but drank the rest of the glass and refilled it anyway. "But I never waste an open bottle."

They didn't talk much after that. The steaks came and his was surprisingly good, or maybe he was just so hungry anything would have tasted fine. She finished everything on her plate and drank the rest of the bottle of wine on her own. When she was done, she picked up her Vuitton bag and went to the restroom. She came back to the table a few minutes later but didn't sit down.

"I took care of the check. Let's get out of here."

Ray looked up at her. "I thought I was taking you to dinner."

"I want to make work off your debt."

He got up and they went back to his room, where he quickly learned that she wasn't kidding. Jerking her off in the pool hadn't taken off any of her edge. She rode him like a Peloton, working up a fine sweat while staring intently at the headboard, maybe biking some steep mountain trail ahead of her, urged on by some imaginary, well-toned trainer instead of Ray's hands clutching her firm ass. But Ray gave as much punishment as he got, taking her just about every way a man could. He decided that it was a good thing that the bed was bolted to the floor.

Afterward, she fell into a deep sleep, snoring away where he'd left her, face-down in the pillows. He was curious about her Vuitton bag, but resisted the urge to unzip it and peek at what she had. Instead, he got out of bed and settled naked and ball-sore into a chair at the table by the window. He positioned himself so he could peek unseen through the edge of the closed drapes at her room across the parking lot, and then picked up the Lee Child novel, reading where he'd left off.

Jack Reacher was also in a motel and peeking out a window. Reacher was also curious about a female guest, though he wasn't fucking her, or even considering the possibility, so Ray couldn't figure out Reacher's interest.

During dinner, Ray had thought about Darlene, her sexy Texas twang, and her dirt-caked Mercedes with the clean California license plates. He added things up and figured she was on the run from something or someone in Texas and, not long before she showed up at the motel, swapped plates with a car from California she found in some parking lot. She was tired but, being cautious, she quickly seduced him because she didn't want to be in her room if whatever she was running from caught up with her.

That was smart, because they showed up at about 2 a.m.

Ray set down the book, turned off the nightstand lamp, and watched two Hispanic men get out of a black Chrysler 300, walk around her car, and go to her door.

One of the men, in baggy black jeans and an untucked shirt, had a snake tattoo that curled around his neck from under his collar, the snake's forked tongue flicking at his earlobe. It was a Vibora cartel tat. He'd seen a few of them in prison. The Snakeman held a Glock down at his side. The other guy, bald and squat and goateed in an over-sized t-shirt and baggy pants, used something to pick the lock, removed a gun from under his shirt, looked back at his partner, then eased open the door. They both raised their guns and slipped inside, one of them kicking the door shut behind them.

Ray thought that Jack Reacher would probably go over there, ask both men what they were up to and, if they gave him any attitude, he'd take their guns, eject the clips, and beat them up. But that's just because, in Ray's opinion, that was what Reacher did to get off instead of fucking. Otherwise, Ray didn't see the point of it.

After a long moment, Snakeman came out, tucked the gun under his shirt, got back into the car, drove out of the lot, and parked across the street, where he could keep an eye on the motel. Ray assumed that Goatee was waiting in the room for Darlene to come back.

Ray got dressed, packed up his things, then returned to the chair. He dozed a bit, but awoke at dawn when a shaft of sunlight hit his face and Darlene stopped snoring. She rolled on her side to check her bag, then smiled at Ray in the chair. He noticed that her breasts were defying gravity, staying firm and upright.

"You lied to me," she said.

"About what?"

"Being easy to please. But thanks for sticking around until I woke up to leave, even though you're obviously in a hurry to go. That's sweet."

"Actually, I'm waiting to go until you shower, brush your teeth, and climb out of the bathroom window. Then I'll get in my car, leave my key at the front desk, and pick you up behind the building."

Darlene looked at him, bewildered. "Why would I want to do that?"

He tipped his head to the draped window beside him. "Your friends are here. One is waiting for you in your room, the other is in a car across the street, watching the motel."

"Fuck." She got up naked, crouched behind him, and peered over his shoulder through the side of the drapes.

"What about my suitcase and car?"

"Forget about them." He was sure that whatever was important to her was in her Vuitton bag. "Do you have a cell phone? She gestured to her big handbag. "In there."

"Is it off?"

"Yeah. I'm not expecting any calls."

"After you've pissed, pull the sim card from the phone and flush it down the toilet. You can toss the phone out once we've hit the road."

Darlene stepped back and looked at him. "Why are you doing this for me?"

Ray wasn't sure he was doing anything for her yet. He might show up behind the motel and he might not. Or he might pick her up but leave her at the next exit. He'd have to wait and see how things shook out. Right now, he was motivated by self-preservation. If she got raped, tortured, kidnapped or killed here, the law would be interested in everyone who'd been at the motel, including him, especially if he'd left right before the deed was done. Too many people had seem them together.

But what he said was: "I wander the country, solving crimes and helping people in trouble."

"That's the book you're reading."

"I told you that it changed my life. Go to the bathroom."

She hesitated, naked in front of him. "How do I know you won't reconsider and leave me behind?"

"Because we made love and now I'm yours."

She grinned and began gathering up her clothes from the floor. "That was fucking, not love-making."

"It's all the same."

"You're probably right. Maybe if I'd realized that before, I might not be in this mess."

She grabbed her bag, went to the bathroom and closed the door. He read a few more chapters of the Reacher novel and, after a few minutes, she opened the bathroom door again and came out.

"Now that I've seen how small that window is," she said, "I wish I didn't eat so much last night."

Ray closed the book and stuffed it into the outside pocket of his little suitcase. "You can fit. Just don't make a lot of noise doing it."

He got up, grabbed his suitcase and room key, and went outside, making sure the door was locked behind him.

He went to his Crown Vic, popped the trunk, dropped the suitcase inside, then walked to the front office. The door was locked and it was dark inside. A hand-written sign, taped to the glass, told guests to drop their key in the mail slot. He did and noticed the reflection of the Chrysler 300 in the glass. Snakeman was in the front seat, watching him. That didn't unnerve Ray. There was nothing else for Snakeman to look at.

Ray went back to his car, got inside, and drove down the street, turned the corner, then went up the alley that ran behind the buildings on the frontage road. Darlene was waiting for him, her bag slung over one shoulder and her high-heeled shoes in one hand. He stopped in front of her. She got into the passenger seat beside him, ducked down without being asked, and he continued down the alley. He got on the Interstate, heading east. Once she felt the car at freeway speeds, she sat up and looked around.

"We're going in the wrong direction."

"Those two knew that you're heading west, so *that's* now the wrong direction."

"I have to get to Los Angeles," she said.

"We can double back that way, just not now, and not on the route you were on before. We'll take the 25 north at Las Cruces to the 40 west and on to L.A."

She thought about that for a minute, then rolled down the window, threw her phone out, then rolled it up again.

Ray asked, "What are you running from?

"An abusive husband. He beats me, rapes me. He'd keep me chained in the cellar if he thought he could get away with it."

He abruptly pulled over to the side of the road, the car fish-tailing as he came to a hard stop. She grabbed the dashboard to steady herself, then glared angrily at him.

"What the fuck is wrong with you?

He reached across her and opened her door. "Get out."

"Why?"

"Because I just saved you from two Vibora *sicarios* and instead of telling me why I could get shot for my trouble, you're lying to me."

"The Viboras. Oh, God. That means it's true." She sunk back into the seat.

"What's true?"

"The rumors around the church about the real reason Chesley's brought so many gang members to Jesus," Darlene said. "They haven't found the Lord. They've found someone to launder their drug money. They give him donations, he gives them bitcoins."

"Who is Chesley?"

"Chesley Upton." She said it like it should mean something to him. It didn't and she noticed, which seemed to irritate her. "The televangelist and motivational speaker. He has a huge Church in Houston and a weekly TV show that's broadcast all over the world."

Now that she'd given him more details, he realized the name was vaguely familiar to him. Some self-help-minded convicts in prison used to watch the show, looking for pointers on how to either turn their lives around or learn the buzz words they needed to convince the parole board that they'd found Jesus.

"Is he the guy with nice suits, the pompadour, the spray-on tan, the pearly-white teeth and a slight overbite?"

She nodded. "I was one of his secretaries for six years. And for the last two, I've been having an affair with him. I thought he loved me, but it turns out we were just fucking." She closed the car door. "Can you start driving again, please? I'll tell you everything. But not while you're looking at me like that."

He pulled back onto the freeway and picked up speed again. "You weren't so shy yesterday."

"That was a different kind of naked. I'm proud of being seen like that. But not like this." She took a deep breath, which Ray worried meant that he was in for a long story. He was.

"Chesley has charisma, he knows how to convince people to believe in him, that he will transform their lives. He certainly did for me. He told me that he loved me. Over and over, passionately. He gave me gifts. Jewelry, clothes, bags, the Mercedes, these breasts. But then Janelle, one of our book keepers, started carrying around a Chanel bag, which she couldn't possibly afford, and then she came back from Easter vacation with a rack just like mine."

"And I'll bet they're just like his wife's, too." Ray glanced at her and saw from her expression that he was right.

"I knew he'd paid for them and that he was never going to leave his wife for me. He'd just create a new sex doll when he got tired of the one he had," Darlene said. "That's all I was to him, a sex doll."

A tear rolled down her cheek, but Ray could tell it wasn't sadness that was making her cry, it was rage.

"I felt so stupid, so used. I went to the church bathroom, locked myself in a stall, and started to cry. That's when God offered me the *Wall Street Journal.*"

"God is selling newspaper subscriptions in bathrooms?"

"It was on the floor. There was an article about a guy in England who'd accidentally thrown away a laptop ten years ago that contained the cryptographic key he needs to access 7500 bitcoins that he bought," she said. "Now he's willing to pay a city millions of dollars to search the trash dump for it. "

Ray didn't know much about bitcoin, except that it was some kind of digital currency. He didn't trust computers. He liked cash, and liked it close, which was a big reason why his was in the door panels of his car and not in a bank. It was a crude system, but he couldn't think of anything better yet.

"What are those coins worth now?"

"$280 million."

"What did that city tell him?"

"To go screw himself, that digging up the dump would create a massive environmental hazard."

Poor bastard, Ray thought. Should have stuck with cash, or gold, or something else of value he could hold in his hands. "Is there a moral to this story?"

"Chesley used to brag to me about all the bitcoins he'd been buying with God's guidance and how they'd exploded in value," she said. "So while Chesley was in the studio, broadcasting his sermon, I stole his laptop from his office and ran away with it."

Now it was all making sense. "How much money does Chesley have locked up in bitcoins?"

"At least a million dollars, maybe more. And most of it is probably the Vibora's money, so they'll cut off his balls if he doesn't get it back."

"Don't you need passwords to access the laptop, use the crypto-key and cash the bitcoin?"

"It's even more complicated than that. But my brother works at Best Buy and knows a guy on the Geek Patrol who found a guy in Los Angeles on the dark web who can do it all and will buy the computer from me for $100,000."

Ray was sure that meant her brother was probably dead and that the Viboras would be waiting for her in Los Angeles. Even if they weren't, the Dark Web guy wouldn't pay her anything. He'd just take the laptop. Her plan was reckless and stupid, driven by anger, not intelligence.

"That's too dangerous and you'll be ripped off."

"It's a chance I have to take," she said. "I can't cash the bitcoin myself."

"The smart move is to sell the laptop back to Chesley."

She stared at him. "He'll kill me."

"No, he won't. You have an edge now you didn't have before."

"What's that?

Ray smiled at her. "Me."

The plan came to Ray in an instant, fully-formed and close to perfect. His biggest problem would be where to find more nooks and crannies in his car to store his share of the cash.

⚜ ⚜ ⚜

Darlene talked almost non-stop during the next seven hours, but Ray tuned most of it out. It was basically a dreary litany of all the bad luck she'd had in her life, growing up poor in a double-wide in Alvin, Texas, and how she'd thought she'd finally found salvation, love, and money with Chesley, only to get screwed over again. Now God was giving her a second chance and she wasn't going to mess it up. She thought she might stay in Los Angeles and use her good looks to pursue a modeling or acting career.

They stopped at a Walmart in Fort Stockton, another bleak, dusty expanse of dry hopelessness.

He used cash to buy four burner phones, a gym bag, a pair of leather gloves, and a laser pointer, as well as some clothes, sensible shoes and toiletries for Darlene.

They were still another eight hours from Houston, and Ray, who hadn't slept much the night before, wanted to get there rested and alert, so he decided they'd stay in Fort Stockton for the night.

Ray checked them into a Holiday Inn Express, using a driver's license and credit card for "David Barer," just in case Chesley and the Viboras had the smarts, and technical resources, to flag any credit card purchases from people who'd been registered at the motel in Helmsby.

They went to their room, used the bathroom, Darlene put on her new shoes, and then they drove across the street to the KBOB Steakhouse for dinner.

She was quiet while they ate, which Ray was thankful for. He'd been tempted to buy a pair of noise-cancelling headphones at Walmart so he could endure the rest of their trip. She didn't speak until they'd finished their meals.

"I'll never mistake fucking for love again. I'm not sure that love even exists." She looked at Ray. "What about you?"

"I don't need to be loved, so it doesn't matter."

"What do you need?"

He'd given that issue a lot of thought when he was in prison and even more thought since he'd become wealthy, which was why he'd found the Reacher novel so helpful. It gave him a foundation he could build upon.

"Independence. A fast, dependable car. Good food. Frequent sex. A good book. Occasional risk."

"Occasional risk? What's that?"

"What I'm doing now."

"I thought you were doing it for me," she said, sounding vaguely hurt, "and for the money."

For the money, maybe, but certainly not for her. But he saw no upside in hurting her feelings. "I am, but I'm also doing it to stay sharp. It's how I survive."

"Is the risk you face always money, injury or death?"

"Sometimes it's losing everything you have *except* your life."

Darlene studied him. "Have you ever lost?"

"Everybody loses."

"How do you find the occasional risk?"

He shrugged. "It usually finds me. Like you did."

She shook her head, rejecting his answer. "I seduced you, but another man would have missed the risk entirely. He would have driven away from the motel this morning, thinking it was his lucky day, and would never have known how unlucky it might have turned out for me. You were waiting and watching for an opportunity and somehow, you sensed the danger I was in. That's what I'm asking about. What did you see that another man might miss?"

"Your desperation."

"Other men would simply have taken advantage of me."

"Isn't that what I'm doing?"

"You didn't throw me out of the car and keep the laptop for yourself."

"It crossed my mind."

She laughed. "At least you're honest about it."

That depended, he thought, on her definition of honesty.

They went back to the Holiday Inn Express and fucked with absolutely no illusions about why they were doing it. He did it because it felt good. She did it because it might be the last night of her life.

⚜ ⚜ ⚜

The next morning in the Crown Vic, on their way into Houston, Darlene called Chesley on one of the burner phones and put him on speaker so Ray could hear the conversation.

The first thing Chesley said was: "Where are you, sweetheart?"

He said it softly, his Texas twang smoother, making his words almost seem like he was singing a song.

"Why?" she asked. "So you can send more gang members to kill me?"

"I sent those boys out to find you and to protect you if you're in trouble. I'm deeply worried about you and your safety. Nothing means more to me than that. Come back, and together we'll purge the evil that's possessed you through prayer, spiritual reflection, and the love of Jesus Christ."

"Don't make me gag, Chesley. All you're worried about are your precious bitcoins and if you want them back, you'll do exactly what I tell you."

"Listen to yourself, Darlene. You're speaking with Satan's voice, not your own." His irritation was beginning to emerge, underscore his words like a new backbeat. "What's happened to the sweet, loving woman I know?"

"She saw Janelle's new tits, you dumb shit. I want two hundred thousand dollars in cash evenly split between two identical gym bags. Meet me for the exchange at 5 p.m. at Goode's BBQ on Kirby Drive, at one of the picnic tables closest to the front."

"I don't have that kind of cash lying around."

"You're forgotten that you once fucked me at the St. Regis on a bed covered with cash."

"It looked like more money than it was. That was maybe five grand," he said dismissively, not exactly helping his argument. "You're asking for a lot more and I don't have it."

"That's a shame, sweetheart. I'll watch the news for your obituary. Rest in peace." She touched a number key, as if she'd missed the disconnect button, and it made a beep.

"Wait!" Chesley practically screamed the word. Ray would have heard him even if the call wasn't on speaker. "Maybe there's a way. The only place I can get that much cash fast is from the funds we use to feed the poor in our kitchen. Can you live with all those children going hungry?"

"You're right. It's heartbreaking. Those starving kids shouldn't have to suffer so you can get your laptop back."

Chesley sighed with relief. "I knew you'd see the light, that you weren't totally lost to the Devil."

"I guess you'll have to sell your Ferrari tomorrow to replenish the account. But think how good it will make you feel."

"Go to hell," he snapped.

"Really? Why? Aren't you the one who preaches every week about the soul-redeeming power of sacrifice?"

"You were an ugly, pathetic little tramp with bad teeth, a flat chest, and no future until I made you into a woman and this is how you thank me for your salvation. You're an ungrateful bitch."

"Yes, I am. Now imagine how the other women you've made will show you their appreciation someday." She ended the call and tossed the phone out the window. "Good luck getting it up now, asshole."

⚜ ⚜ ⚜

The Goode Company Barbecue on Kirby Drive in central Houston was designed to resemble an enormous barn. There were stacks of mesquite wood out front and several long picnic tables were arranged in rows under an overhang on the north side of the building. There were security cameras everywhere, which was one reason why Ray and Darlene had chosen the restaurant for the exchange.

At 4:15, Ray arrived alone in the Crown Vic and parked in the lot behind the restaurant. He emerged from the car wearing a baseball cap and sunglasses to obscure his face from the cameras. He wore a collared-shirt, leather gloves, and a gym bag over his shoulder. The air was thick with the aroma of cooked meat and mesquite smoke and it made his stomach growl.

Lowering his head, so the cap's bill covered his face, he walked across the patio and into the restaurant. There were only a few table and all of the food on offer, the meat on carving boards and the other dishes in hot trays, was laid out on display buffet-style behind a glass counter. A few customers slid their trays along a shelf in front of the counter and pointed out the food they wanted to the serving staff, their aprons smeared with grease and barbecue sauce.

He picked up a tray, napkins and silverware, snagged a long-necked beer bottle from the ice box, and ordered pork ribs, brisket, beans, cheese bread, and pecan pie. He paid the cashier, walked out to the patio with his tray of full of food, and went to a center picnic table and took a seat that faced busy Kirby Drive. There was a car wash and an apartment complex across the street.

There were only a seven other people outside eating at that hour, and they were widely spread among the tables. None of the diners paid any attention to him.

He took a hoody and a laser pointer out of the shoulder bag and set both items on the table, the hoody hiding the laser pointer, and then, without taking off his gloves, he dug into his early dinner. It was delicious, well worth the drive to Houston on its own. Maybe, he thought, he should decide where to go next based on what food he liked to eat. He'd always enjoyed a bucket of chicken from Colonel Sanders. Maybe he should go to Kentucky to sample the chicken and biscuits there.

He was in middle of that thought, and finishing off his fourth spare rib, when a guy with a snake tattoo around his neck took a seat at one of the picnic tables in front. In Ray's peripheral vision, to his right, he saw another Vibora sit down at the far end of a picnic table, a position that allowed the gang member to cover the alley that ran along the northside of the restaurant. Ray assumed another Vibora was getting in position at the back of the patio, near the parking lot. The stage was being set. The star would be making his entrance soon.

Ray set down his rib, wiped his mouth and gloves with a napkin, and slipped his right hand under the hoody, tenting it up just a bit. A moment later, Chesley appeared on Kirby Drive, lugging a heavy gym bag in each hand, his famous face obscured with a baseball cap, the size sticker still on the bill, and sunglasses. He wore a polo shirt, khaki slacks and topsiders, and sat down at the same front table as the Vibora, but pretended not to notice him.

Ray used his free hand to take a bite of the cheese bread and was surprised that it had a little kick to it. Jalapenos. Nice.

A Prius with an Uber sticker on the windshield pulled up to the curb. Darlene was in the backseat. Ray knew she was telling the young, Hispanic driver to wait, that she'd only be a minute. She got out and approached Chesley, who was clearly pissed off.

Ray couldn't hear their conversation, but he'd written her part of the script and could read their body language, so he basically knew what was going down.

"You didn't come alone," Darlene said, glancing at the Vibora at the end of the table. "Uh-oh. Should I feel threatened?"

"I don't see my laptop."

"It's already here with a friend." She tipped her head to Ray, who flicked on the laser pointer under the hoody, putting a pinprick red target on Chesley's chest. "He's holding a laser-targeted gun fitted with a suppressor. He'll shoot you if he thinks I'm in any kind of jeopardy."

Chesley glanced at Ray, then at the spot over his heart, then back at Darlene. The preacher's face was red with anger, a vein pulsing in his forehead. Ray hoped the guy wouldn't have a stroke.

Darlene continued. "But we're all being watched on security cameras out here, so we wouldn't want that to happen, would we?" Chesley noticed the cameras in the eaves of the restaurant. "Try to resist the urge to face the camera and ask for donations."

He turned to her. "Fuck you."

She grinned. "Actually, I'm the one doing the fucking here, Chesley, and this might be the first time I don't have to fake my pleasure with you. Open the bags and show me the cash."

Chesley lifted each bag onto the table and unzipped them a crack so she could see the cash. She reached inside each one to thumb through some of the packets to make sure they weren't stacks of paper with a real bill on top for show. While she did that, Ray smiled at each of the two Viboras giving him death stares and took a sip of his beer. Darlene, satisfied, zipped up the bags.

"Here's what's going to happen next. I'm going to leave with one of these bags. I've got friends watching to see if I'm followed." That was a lie, of course, but Chesley couldn't be sure of that. "Once I'm convinced there are no tracking devices in the bag, and I am a safe distance away, I'll call my friend over there, who will exchange the laptop for the second bag of cash."

She took one of the bags. Chesley grabbed her wrist.

"How do I know that it's my laptop he has or that it hasn't been erased?"

"Have faith, Chesley. That should be easy for you."

She yanked her arm free, smiled at Ray with genuine gratitude, and got into the Uber again. The car drove off. This was good-bye. They had no plans to ever talk or meet again.

Now came the tricky part for Ray. Chesley and the Viboras all shifted their cold gazes to him. Ray used his free hand to eat the rest of the bread. It was damn good. He washed it down with some beer and had a few spoonful's of beans. He wasn't used to eating with his left hand, so he had to be careful not to dribble anything on his shirt.

The Vibora to his right moved to a table closer to Ray, who wagged his spoon at him, signaling that he was being a bad boy. Ray set down the spoon, slid the laptop out of the gym bag, set it on the table and, while looking at the Vibora, tipped the open beer bottle over the keyboard, just enough for the fluid to start down the long neck. The Vibora actually hissed, but moved back to where he'd been sitting before.

Ray set the bottle down and gave him a smile. He pretended that the burner phone had buzzed in his shirt pocket. He took the phone out, dialed 911, and held it to his ear. When the operator answered, he whispered frantically:

"I'm outside Goode's barbecue on Kirby. There are three men here with snake tattoos ... I overheard them say they are going to rob the place. Oh my God, they've got guns ... .and they're looking at me."

He hung up, put the phone in his pocket, and waved Chesley over. There was a police station two miles southwest from the restaurant and another one three miles northeast. Ray was confident that officers would be there within the next three minutes.

Chesley picked up the bag, walked up to Ray's table and set the bag down in front of him. Ray decided it would be fun to stick a knife in him, figuratively speaking. He said, "Thank you for Darlene's new tits and now for all this money. You've been so good to us."

Chesley took the laptop and powered it up. "How long have you been fucking her?"

"Since she turned sixteen."

One of Chesley's eyelids twitched. He typed something on the keyboard and seemed relieved by what he saw on screen. He closed the laptop, nodded to the nearest Vibora and then smiled at Ray.

"You're going to repent for your sins. I think it's going to be painful."

Chesley started to walk back toward Kirby Drive. That's when a Houston PD black-and-white skidded to a stop on the street and another one charged up the alley. Four uniformed officers, their guns drawn, leapt out of their cars. The Vibora nearest Ray, acting on reflex, whirled around and drew his gun.

That's when the shooting started.

Ray grabbed the bag of cash and ducked under his picnic table. He looped the straps of the gym bag over his shoulders like a backpack and started crawling under the tables towards the parking lot. He heard screaming, gunfire, wailing and crying. As he scrambled out from the covered patio, and edged around the back of the building, he saw a Vibora on the ground, twitching as he bled out.

Ray stood up and, without looking back, walked slowly to his car, tossed the bag onto the passenger seat, and drove off.

He wished he'd been able to leave with some more of that cheese bread.

⚜ ⚜ ⚜

Forty minutes later, he was heading east on the 90 Freeway, just past Dayton, when the burner phone vibrated in his pocket. He'd forgotten to turn it off. That was a big mistake. A live phone could be used to track him.

Ray took the phone from his pocket and checked the screen. He'd received a text. It was probably spam, but out of curiosity, he tapped the text notification and a photo of Darlene appeared. She was naked and duct-taped to a chair. Her face was bloody and swollen and a man, his face hidden behind a balaclava, held a gun to her head. Next came a simple text message:

Bring us the money or we'll blow her brains out.

Jack Reacher would have gone back, rescued the girl, and killed the men with his bare hands. But Ray didn't have Reacher's moral code and Darlene was already dead. He thought it was a shame, but her grisly fate was the result of her bad choices. He was making a good choice, and staying alive, by doing nothing about it.

Ray turned off the phone, pulled over to the shoulder, and broke the device apart. Then he started driving again, throwing pieces of the phone out the window over the next few miles. Worried that he might have been tracked by the Viboras or the police, he took the 61 south at Devers, until he hit the westbound Interstate 10 and then headed back to Houston. It was the last place anybody would expect him to be and it was much easier to disappear in a big city.

⚜ ⚜ ⚜

That night, registered as "Frank Kales" in a Doubletree at the Galleria mall in Houston, Ray listened to the late news on TV while examining the bag full of cash that Chesley had given him.

There were two bullet holes in the back of the bag and six packets of cash inside, worth roughly $10,000, had been obliterated by the slugs. That was a surprise. A Vibora must have shot at him as he was crawling away, but he'd never felt a thing.

What wasn't a surprise, though, was that the bag was fifty grand light. Chesley had ripped them off, gambling that Darlene wouldn't stick around to count the cash before handing over the laptop. But Chesley had lost in the end.

The top story on TV was the evangelist's violent death in a bloody gang shooting at a barbecue place that had also left three Viboras, one cop, and two bystanders dead. Ray wondered if identifying the blood spatter from all the barbecue sauce everywhere would be a challenge for the CSI people.

He knew the laptop exchange was recording on security video, but he was confident, because he'd been wearing gloves, that he hadn't left any fingerprints behind and he doubted anybody would analyze the table scraps on the ground for DNA.

The news rambled on, but there was no mention of Darlene's fate, not that he'd expected any. Her body might not be found for days or weeks, if ever. He wondered, though, if her brother's body had been discovered yet and if the police would make the connection between the two murders.

Ray switched from the news to one of the hotel's porn channels, arriving in time to see a lesbian gang-bang. He didn't get aroused by porn, but he found it relaxing in the same way that some people liked home renovation shows. And, like watching those shows, he occasionally picked up some practical information. But tonight the porn was just on for company, a little white, sapphic noise to fill his empty room.

All things considered, he decided it had been a good day. He was alive, he'd had a delicious lunch, made some good money, and he was in a comfortable room. He'd even been given a hot, chocolate chip cookie at check-in.

He laid on the bed, opened the Reacher novel, and started reading, with no idea where he'd go tomorrow.

ABOUT THE AUTHOR

Lee Goldberg is a two-time Edgar Award and two-time Shamus Award finalist and the #1 *New York Times* bestselling author of more than forty novels, including the *Eve Ronin* series, the *Ian Ludlow* series, and the first five books in the *Fox & O'Hare* series, which he coauthored with Janet Evanovich. He has also written and/or produced many TV shows, including *Diagnosis Murder*, *SeaQuest*, and *Monk*, and is the cocreator of the Hallmark movie series *Mystery 101*. As an international television consultant, he has advised networks and studios in Canada, France, Germany, Spain, China, Sweden, and the Netherlands on the creation, writing, and production of episodic series. You can find more information about Lee and his work at www.leegoldberg.com.

Printed in Great Britain
by Amazon